"MY BABY!
HE'S STILL IN THERE!"

Just then, the building was rocked by an explosion.
Flames shot high in the air. The woman, horrified,
tried to go back to the building. The firemen restrained her.

"No one can go in there now," the Fire Chief told
her. "It's too dangerous." Someone in the crowd
shouted and pointed up. "What's that?" A searchlight found a figure poised on the roof of the building next door. He wore no mask or cape, but the
red, blue and gold costume was unmistakable.

"IT'S CAPTAIN AVENGER!"

He backed up, then ran forward and leaped from
roof to roof. Then he entered the burning building.
Walls were sagging, ceilings broken. There was an
ominous creaking sound. The building seemed to
sway slightly. A cry came from somewhere. He
turned in its direction. Suddenly he looked into the
dirty, tear-stained face of a boy. The child looked
at his rescuer in wonder. "Captain Avenger!"

Then the flames engulfed them both.

METRO-GOLDWYN-MAYER

Presents

JOHN RITTER
ANNE ARCHER

in

"HERO AT LARGE"
A STEPHEN FRIEDMAN/KINGS ROAD PRODUCTION

Starring
BERT CONVY
KEVIN McCARTHY

Associate Producer
ROGER M. ROTHSTEIN

Director of Photography
DAVID M. WALSH

Music by
PATRICK WILLIAMS

Written by
A. J. CAROTHERS

Produced by
STEPHEN FRIEDMAN

Directed by
MARTIN DAVIDSON

METROCOLOR®
© 1979 Metro-Goldwyn-Mayer Inc.

HERO AT LARGE

A. J. CAROTHERS

48

80 2814 8

BALLANTINE BOOKS • NEW YORK

Library of Congress Catalog Card Number: 79-92624

ISBN 0-345-28383-X

Manufactured in the United States of America

First Edition: February 1980

2108242

Chapter
One

HIS powerful body shaping a red, blue and gold costume, a lightning bolt bent into an "A" insignia on his broad chest, a mask sleek on his upper face —Captain Avenger sailed across Times Square. His cleft chin was set boldly forward. One muscular arm was extended, the hand doubled into a massive fist, ready for action.

No one paid much attention. There were a few curious glances. One child pointed. A woman laughed. For the most part, people kept to their own business, eyes straight ahead, hurrying, pushing.

A young violinist stood on the corner of Broadway and Forty-seventh Street, playing something by Bach. A man on skates rolled past, carrying an open umbrella and wearing a sign that read "Hi. My name is Roy." No one paid much attention to them either.

Captain Avenger turned onto Forty-fifth and was stopped by crosstown traffic. The bus carrying the forty-foot papier-mâché figure was, like the hero himself, a relic of the nineteen forties. It had been spruced up for this job, painted bright yellow and plastered with glittering stars. But it was old and tired. It stalled in the crosswalk. While its motor struggled to turn over, loudspeakers at its front and rear blared a recorded message: "Captain Avenger

3

is coming your way! The superhero who thrilled a generation returns to rock the motion picture screen with new excitement."

The message was lost in the honking of impatient motorists caught behind the stalled bus. An angry cabbie leaned out of his taxi and gave Captain Avenger the finger.

Steve and Denise, walking up Eighth Avenue, reached Forty-fifth as the bus shuddered and coughed and started to move again, it's loudspeakers trailing the promise: "This weekend, Captain Avenger appears in person at a theater near you." The two young people didn't hear it, involved as they were in a tense discussion.

"How did it happen?"

"You knocked me up, that's how."

Steve threw her an accusing look. "You said you were safe."

"I was wrong."

"It's a hell of a thing to be wrong about!" Steve shouldered his way through a knot of people, momentarily leaving Denise behind. She hurried to catch up.

"Excuse me," she said sarcastically, "but you're not taking this too well."

"I'm sorry."

"So am I. I'm the one that's knocked up."

A traffic signal stopped them at Forty-sixth. Steve turned to look at her and his expression softened. Thin and pale, her eyes too large for her face, Denise was a waif, lost and vulnerable. "What are you going to tell your folks?"

Denise stared blankly.

"What are you going to tell your folks?" he repeated.

"Shit!" She rummaged in a huge macrame shoulder bag to produce a tattered script. "I had this scene cold."

Steve shook his head helplessly. "Nevermind. We'll go over it another time."

"No. Please. It was going so well." Denise flipped pages, looking for the forgotten line. "Wasn't it going well?"

"Yeah, it was fine. But I've got to go now. I'm meeting my agent."

"When can we do it? Monday before class?"

"Sure." Seeing a break in the traffic, Steve dashed out into the street.

Denise called anxiously after him. "You won't forget."

Steve looked back over his shoulder to assure her. "I won't forget." Then, from the opposite curb, he yelled "Learn your lines!"

He stopped at a newsstand to buy the new issue of *Show Business*. As he started walking again, he turned to the casting pages and noted upcoming auditions and interviews.

"*The Grand Tour*, music and lyrics by Jerry Herman, book by Michael Stewart and Mark Bramble, needs immediate chorus replacements. Male and female singers who can move. All types. Small parts will be cast from the chorus."

Steve frowned thoughtfully. He couldn't really call himself a singer, though he'd had some lessons and he wasn't tone deaf or anything. No problem about moving. He might give it a shot. He wondered if any of those small parts were worthwhile.

"Interviews will be held for the following roles in *Shadow Box*, to be directed by Richard Cham-

berlain and performed at the Charles Playhouse in
Boston. . . ."

Steve's eyes covered the cast breakdown. They
were all middle-aged characters. Except the part
of Mark. Mid-twenties. Handsome. The age was
perfect. What about handsome? He glanced at
himself in a store window. Nice-looking, yes. But
handsome? He shrugged. Maybe nice-looking would
be enough.

Cyrano de Bergerac. An off-Broadway production. All parts open.

Steve broke into a smile. He did Cyrano in high
school. What a part! What a play!

There were a dozen things worth checking out,
with a little stretch here, a little luck there. In
Steve Nichols, hope sprang eternal. It always had.
Back in Cawker City, Kansas, he was the kid who
went out for football when he was fifteen pounds
underweight, ran for class president against the
biggest hotshot in school and asked the most
popular girl to the prom. At Kansas State, he was
nicknamed "Gofer" because he would always "go
fer it." Failure didn't stop him. Disappointment
didn't sour him. Even three years in New York
couldn't get him down.

He folded *Show Business*, stuck it in the pocket
of his corduroy jacket and breezed into the Gaiety
Delicatessen. Steve liked the Gaiety. Because it
was popular with theater people, there were always friends to greet and occasionally a celebrity
to ogle. Steve had not outgrown ogling. Once when
he saw Woody Allen he had to take his food home
in a doggie bag, unable to eat in such a presence.

Marty Fields was sitting at a table in the middle
of the restaurant section, ordering a corned beef

on rye. Steve came up behind him, leaned close to his ear and declared with fervor, "I'm a storm, a flame!"

Marty was unperturbed. "You want a sandwich?"

Steve walked around the table, gesturing dramatically. "Too strong to war with mortals, bring me giants!"

"Bring him a corned beef sandwich."

The waiter nodded and walked away, as Steve dropped into a chair opposite his agent. "Marty, there's an off-Broadway production of *Cyrano*."

"That's nice."

"I know that play by heart."

"What about the beer commercial?"

A small, balding man with a permanently pained expression that came from a general dissatisfaction with the world, and from chronic gastritis, Marty had been Steve's agent for two years. He understood Steve's dreams. He had represented dozens of young dreamers through the years. But he was a practical man. An actor is somebody who acts, preferably for money. Maybe someday it would be *Hamlet* for Steve, or *Cyrano de Bergerac*. But for now, there was nothing wrong with a beer commercial.

Steve shrugged indifferently. "I read for them this morning."

"And?"

"They liked my sincerity."

"How'd they like your acting?"

"How much can you do with 'That's what I call beer!' Marty, please." Steve clasped his hands together in supplication. "Get me a play. Any play."

"It's not like you never did one. Last summer, Shakespeare in the Park."

Steve laughed. "I carried a spear. Jesus, Marty, that's a joke. When an actor says he carried a spear, he doesn't mean he carried a spear. *I* carried a spear!"

Jerry Feldman saw Steve from the door, went directly to the table, fell to his knees and bent forward until his forehead touched the floor. "Oh, most worthy person," he chanted. "Prince of actors, friend of friends."

Marty looked down at this performance with the aplomb of someone who has seen everything and asked, "Who's the Arab?"

Steve indicated one, then the other. "Jerry Feldman, Marty Fields."

Jerry got to his feet, shook hands with Marty, then looked back at Steve. "I got it. The Schlitz commercial."

"Hey, that's great." Steve was genuinely pleased, breaking into a wide grin and raising his first in an enthusiastic "right on" gesture.

"You're what's great. I wouldn't have even known about it if you hadn't told me."

Marty looked back and forth, incredulous.

"I won't forget you," Jerry promised. "Honest to God. You'll be in my will." He gave Steve a big kiss on the forehead, then left as quickly as he had come.

For a long moment, Marty just looked at Steve, as if he couldn't find words. When he finally did speak, it was in a quiet, controlled voice. "You told him about the beer commercial."

"He's in my acting class. Really a good guy."

"You told him and he got it."

"He needed a break."

Marty's voice was suddenly loud. "Schmuck!"

"He'll do the same for me sometime."

"You believe that? *Double* schmuck!"

"Come on, Marty, *you* didn't lose the commercial."

"Do I get ten percent from the Arab?" Marty pulled a handkerchief out of his pocket and mopped his brow.

Steve smiled at that age-old expression of exasperation and thought to himself that everybody's an actor. Then he became serious again. "Get me a play, Marty."

"I'll get you a head examiner."

The waiter put two corned beef sandwiches on the table. Marty looked up at him. "Did you put these on separate checks?"

"No, I put 'em on rye, like you said."

Marty threw up his hands. "A schmuck and a smart ass. I'm surrounded!"

Steve laughed. "Relax, Marty. I'll buy you a sandwich."

"With what? An unemployed actor."

Steve leaned across the table and spoke in a hushed, psuedosecretive tone. "At night, I'm Captain Avenger."

Marty snorted. "A pair of do-gooders. Neither *one* of you makes any money."

Chapter Two

NIGHT. An area near the docks. A dark figure dashed across the flat roof of a warehouse, lept to an adjacent one-story building and crouched by a skylight, a startling apparition in yellow light from below. Captain Avenger. His jaw tightened at what he saw through streaked, dirty glass. An elderly scientist and his female assistant, shapely even in her laboratory smock, were tied to chairs, threatened by two grim-faced thugs. One of them held a Bunsen burner close to the assistant's pretty face.

Captain Avenger made a careful judgment, stood and jumped feet-first through the skylight. Thugs and victims looked up, astonished, as the unexpected visitor landed neatly on a laboratory table. "Mind if I drop in?" he asked with a teasing smile.

"Get him!" ordered the thug with the burner. His companion moved toward the intruder, pulling a gun. A gold boot caught him under the chin and sent him sprawling.

In a flash, Captain Avenger jumped to the floor, grabbed the man with the burner and hit him with a jaw-crushing right.

"We're saved!" the assistant cried, her eyes filled with gratitude and admiration.

"Thank God," said the scientist. "You got here just in time."

Steve was chinning himself on a steel bar bolted into the doorway between a tiny kitchen and the living room-bedroom-gymnasium he called home. His attention, when his eyes dropped below the door frame, was fastened on the Captain Avenger commercial.

"Sworn to uphold justice, protect the weak and punish wrongdoers, Captain Avenger fights a never-ending battle against the forces of evil." The announcer's voice throbbed with excitement.

Steve pulled himself up again and again, counting silently, each repetition taking more effort. Perspiration ran down his face and neck. His torso glistened. The waistband of his sweat pants was soaked.

On the television screen, a series of scenes from the movie showed Captain Avenger in action, slugging villains, saving victims, meeting danger with cool panache.

"This is his story." Music swelled behind the announcer's voice. "His greatest adventure."

In the last cut, Captain Avenger stood tall, legs apart, hands on hips, to ask the question that was his trademark: "Who says nice guys finish last?" He smiled, confident, blue eyes sparkling. The comic-book hero supreme.

Steve finished his count, dropped to the floor and struck the same pose, tried the same smile.

As the commercial ended, a local announcer added hurriedly that Captain Avenger would be appearing in person at selected theaters and urged viewers to check their newspapers for times and locations.

Steve grabbed a towel to wipe his face and neck, then crossed to the TV set, stepping over a slant board and some dumbbells. The one-room apartment was a shrine to clutter, books and records stacked on tables and chairs, photographs, theater programs and newspaper clippings tacked haphazardly to the walls, a bicycle in the corner, gym equipment everywhere. Actually, the mess added personality to what was just another single apartment in another old building in the West Village.

Steve flipped the selector switch, stopping on a scene from an old movie. He stood back, watching Gable and Crawford face each other in a sleazy South American hotel.

Gable was talking, tough and cocksure. "I don't know about tomorrow, but tonight you're the most beautiful woman in the world. Does that mean anything to you?"

"Not much." Crawford was tough too.

Smiling, Steve backed away from the screen into the kitchen, where he put some milk and a spoon of high-protein mix into a blender. He kept looking over his shoulder at the movie. He liked old movies. Especially Gable. What a guy! He set the blender whirring and moved back toward the TV, started to pick up a pair of dumbbells but saw something through the front window that took his attention away from exercises, from Gable, from everything.

Jolene Marsh, the young woman walking toward the building, had the kind of freewheeling good looks you see on billboards: long and lean, with great legs. She was carrying a large potted plant.

Steve looked around for something to put on, pulled a T-shirt out of an open laundry package and dashed out of the apartment, not bothering to close the door. In the hall, he pulled the shirt over his head as he hurried toward the entrance. Rounding a corner, he stopped by a row of mailboxes, casually looking up when Jolene came in, as if he just happened to be there.

Working around her plant, trying to keep its leaves out of her face, Jolene found a key in her handbag and unlocked her mailbox. Steve kept looking, but the object of his interest didn't seem to notice. "So you're J. Marsh." He said it with a trace of Gable swagger. "I'm S. Nichols. We're neighbors."

"Hello." She gave him one quick glance, then turned back to her mailbox. She was having trouble because of the plant.

Steve shrugged off the Gable bit. "You want me to hold that for you?"

Jolene looked at him for a moment before handing it over. "Thanks." She took several things out of her mailbox and sifted through them.

"I've seen you come and go a few times."

She shot him another look, on guard.

"I live in the front apartment."

"And you watch people come and go."

"I'm an actor. So, I watch people."

"Haven't you got it backwards?"

Steve smiled at that. "I learn things. About how people are, you know?"

"How are they?"

Steve decided to take the plunge. "Well—*you* look sort of lonely."

"I'm not." She dropped her mail in her handbag and reached out to take the plant.

"That's okay," Steve smiled, peering at her through the leaves. "We're going in the same direction."

"What about *your* mail?"

"Huh? Oh. I forgot my key."

She nodded knowingly. "Must have left your apartment in a hurry."

They started walking along the hall. An effort had been made to brighten it. The walls were painted yellow. Doors and wood trim were orange. It was a lost cause. Some places are dreary, no matter what. It's built-in.

Steve kept the conversation going, trying to cut through his neighbor's surface cool. "Did you move here from out of town?"

"No."

"Somewhere in the city. Queens?"

"East Sixty-sixth Street."

"Yeah?" His surprise showed. East Sixty-sixth was a very fancy neighborhood.

"Why would anybody move here from there, right?"

"No." He tried to cover. "I wasn't thinking that."

"You're a lousy liar, for an actor."

As they passed Steve's door, he reacted to the strained whirring of his blender. "My Tiger Shake!" he cried, dashing into his apartment.

"My scheffleral" She followed him.

Steven switched off the blender, then turned with an apologetic smile. "I do that all the time."

She was looking around the apartment in a vaguely curious way.

"This is it," Steve shrugged. "Home sweet home."

"It looks like a gym."

"I have to stay in shape. I take a lot of lessons too. Voice, movement, fencing—"

"Do you ever act?" She said it casually, but she was being tough.

"Well, sure." He thought of Joan Crawford.

"Professionally?" She dug right in there.

"Sometimes." What would Gable do? Probably sock her.

"What do you do other times?"

"Whatever. I drive relief cab."

She nodded, getting the picture. "May I have my plant now?"

"I'll deliver it to your door."

"You'd better have your drink."

"It has to settle."

She wanted to get rid of him. He knew that. She figured he wasn't worth her time. But he wasn't going to make it easy. They went back into the hall.

"What do you do?" Steve asked casually.

"About what?"

"I act. What do *you* do?"

"I make commercials."

"Hey, so do I." Maybe they had something in common after all, something he could use to get her interest. "I've got one running right now—"

"Other side of the camera."

They reached her door. She turned to take the plant.

"I guess you have a date tonight."

"No."

Steve brightened.

"I'm working."

"That's perfect," he grinned. "I am too. Till about ten."

"As a cabbie?"

"As an actor." He was glad he could come back with that. "How about after?"

"We start at eleven."

Steve frowned curiously.

"It's the only time we can get into Sardi's."

"That's where you're working?"

She nodded wearily. "Sparky Goes to Opening Night."

"Sparky the Dog? You do those commercials."

"God help me." She stepped into her apartment.

"Maybe some other time," he said quickly, "when you're not working."

She looked at him for a moment. "I don't think so."

"Why not?" It was a risky question, but what did he have to lose?

"You live in a lousy neighborhood." She smiled as she closed the door.

Steve just stood there, thoughtful. She wasn't exactly a pushover. But it was nothing personal. She didn't know him. The way she smiled— Hope was springing eternal.

Chapter
Three

IT was a perfect spring night, the kind of weather that gets people out of the house. Even so, the crowd gathered outside the Elmwood Theater in Queens was of modest size. It was mostly children with their parents, a few older kids on their own. The center of their attention was a man in a tight red, blue and gold costume, a mask across his upper face. It was Captain Avenger, as played by Steve Nichols. This was the acting job he had mentioned to Jolene Marsh.

A boy about nine years old, urged on by his father, came forward to get an autograph. "Does it hurt when some crook socks you in the face?"

"Sure it does." Steve was playing the part with all the truth he could bring to it, smiling the Captain Avenger smile, using a firm Captain Avenger voice. "I'm just a man, except maybe I'm stronger than most and I don't scare off easy."

Eddie Pierce, the public relations man at Steve's side, looked at him with open wonder.

"I don't believe you," he whispered to Steve after the boy had turned away. "The way you keep dishing out that stuff."

"It's right for the character."

Three boys in their early teens, dressed in tight pants and leather jackets, swaggered up to them.

"Hey, Captain Avenger," one of the teenagers baited, "let's see you fly."

Steve looked at the three boys, knew they were troublemakers, but tried to play it straight. "Sorry, I don't fly."

A second teenager poked his friend, a cocky smile on his face. "Don't let him shit you, man. Anybody dresses like that flies."

"You mean he's a fruit?"

They laughed and punched at each other.

"You saw the picture, man. He don't fool around with girls. They're fallin' all over him and he don't do nothin'."

The third teenager moved closer to Steve. "Hey, can I feel your muscle?" He struck a provocative pose. "I'll let you feel *mine*."

"You faggot!" The first boy made smacking noises with his lips. There was more laughing and punching.

Eddie moved toward them, anxious to end this confrontation before it got out of hand. "Okay, you guys move on and let some of the younger kids get in closer."

"*You* wanna feel my muscle?"

"I wanna kick your butt."

"Take it easy," Steve urged him. "The others can hear."

The three boys circled Steve and Eddie from a safe distance, considering what to do next.

A little girl came forward, pushy and impertinent. "If you're really Captain Avenger, why aren't you out chasing crooks?"

Steve was at a loss for words.

A boy, slight of build, wearing glasses and

24

braces, moved to Captain Avenger's defense. "He's got a night off." He looked at Steve. "Right?"

Steve smiled. "Right. So I can meet some people."

One of the teenagers stepped in to take another shot. "Hey, Captain Fruit, the little kid wants to feel you."

Steve's expression darkened. He made a move for the boy, who gave a whoop and took off.

"Here comes the bus," Eddie declared gratefully.

The yellow bus with the colossal Captain Avenger on top approached the theater, its loudspeakers blaring spirited music from the movie soundtrack.

Eddie moved in front of Steve, clearing the way. "Okay, boys and girls, we've got to go now."

Steve paused to rumple the slight boy's hair. "So long, sport."

As he and Eddie reached the bus, air-pressure doors opened. Eddie handed over a folded trench coat. "Here's your coat. I'll see you tomorrow."

Steve nodded and stepped into the bus, turned for a last wave to the crowd and called out boldly, "Who says nice guys finish last?"

"Jesus," said Eddie. "You never give up."

The air doors closed with a hiss.

In the bus, Steve looked around at twenty other Captain Avengers, talking, smoking. Their masks were off. Some were bootless. He took a seat near the front, next to a young man who glanced up from *Variety*.

"How's it going?" Steve smiled.

"Don't ask. Two years at Actors Studio for *this?*"

Steve shrugged. "It's like any other part. You

have to really get into it. At that theater, I *was* Captain Avenger."

"Listen, I gave it a shot. And I was doing okay, until this kid got me with a pellet gun."

Steve looked at him in astonishment.

The actor nodded. "Right in the ass. Wanted to know if I was really tough."

"What did you do?"

"I screamed. I'm not tough. Not in the ass."

Steve sat back in his seat, genuinely disturbed. "What's happened to kids?" he wondered. "When I was growing up, back in Cawker City, Kansas, we believed in heroes. John Wayne. And Davy Crockett. When they finally got that coonskin cap off of me, they had to bury it."

"I was a 'Dragnet' freak," the young actor reminisced, suddenly wistful.

"Only the facts, ma'm."

"An honest cop."

"Polite."

They both sat there, smiling, nostalgic. Then Steve's companion pulled himself out of it. "You can't expect people to buy that kind of stuff today," he said flatly, and went back to his *Variety*.

Steve sighed, "It's too bad." He meant it. It *was* too bad. There was no one to look up to anymore, no one to idealize and emulate. Sports stars were traded from team to team, loyal only to their bank accounts. Presidents and congressmen were accused of crimes, forced to resign their offices. Steve tried to think of a current hero. He couldn't. It depressed him.

A few minutes later, he looked to the front of the bus, past the driver, and realized he was near home. He got up and, pulling on his trench coat, went to stand just behind the driver. He bent down to look through the windshield.

"Could you let me off at Sheridan Square?"

"Whadya think this is," the driver snapped, "a limo?"

"Come on. If I go uptown, I have to take a taxi all the way back. That's four bucks."

"Try the subway."

The bus stopped for a red light. Steve hit the lever that opened the air-pressure doors. "Thanks a lot," he called to the angry driver as he jumped off the bus.

Steve walked briskly. His trench coat was belted over the Captain Avenger costume, the collar buttoned high. The gold boots were exposed, but they weren't too conspicuous in the darkness. No one gave him a second look.

He turned down a deserted side street, whistling to himself, paused to look at a poster that featured a familiar figure in a dynamic action pose. A word had been crudely added so the sign read "Captain Avenger sucks."

Steve grimaced at the grafitti, then walked on. He passed a small corner grocery, got a thought and backed up. Mr. Rothberg, the owner, was just hanging a sign on the door—"Closed."

Steve put his lips close to the glass. "I just need some milk."

Rothberg considered a moment, then opened up.

"Thanks," Steve smiled. "I appreciate it."

"The milk's in back."

Steve went to a refrigerator at the rear of the store, while Rothberg joined his wife behind a counter at one side of the store. She was checking the register, counting in German.

The door opened again and two boys in their late teens entered. One stayed by the door, considering a Manischewitz wine display, while his companion went to pick up a six-pack of beer. He set it on the counter.

"Something else?" Rothberg asked. He was anxious to close.

"Yeah." The young man glanced at his companion. "You got a bag?"

Rothberg produced a paper bag, popped it open and reached for the six-pack. "That's $1.80."

"Not the beer," the boy snarled. "The cash."

"Come again?"

"You heard me."

The boy put his closed hand on the counter and pressed a button. An evil-looking blade snapped into place, like a striking snake.

"My God!" Mrs. Rothberg moved toward her husband.

"Watch it, lady," the punk warned. "You make a move, I'll cut off your nose."

Steve was bent down, reaching to the back of a low shelf, when he heard the threat. He straightened, incredulous. The scene at the cash register was reflected in the glass doors of the big refrigerator.

"Okay, old man, let's have it," the punk with the switchblade commanded. His companion pulled the shade on the door so they couldn't be seen from the street.

Without turning, Steve quietly stepped to the side, putting himself behind a standing soft-drink display.

Rothberg opened the cash register and started putting money in the paper bag, but then he stopped and looked again at the threatening teenager. "Think what you're doing," he urged.

The kid, getting nervous, made a sudden move with the knife. "You want me to make a slice?"

"No!" Mrs. Rothberg cried. She begged her husband to give him the money.

Suddenly, a dashing figure stepped into the open, masked, ready for action. His sudden move, complete with theatrical gesture, upset the drink display, which toppled over, cans and bottles crashing to the floor. Robbers and victims alike turned, astonished.

"Holy shit!" the punk with the knife exclaimed.

Steve stepped back, momentarily thrown by the collapse of the display, but quickly recovered with a cocky Captain Avenger smile.

"Mind if I break in?"

Mr. Rothberg couldn't believe his eyes. "It's Captain Avenger."

The second punk jumped into action, grabbed the paper bag from Rothberg and threw open the door. Steve rushed forward and made a flying tackle. The kid sprawled on the floor. The bag ripped and the money scattered. Scrambling away from Steve, the kid got to his feet and ran like hell.

Steve stood now between the kid with the knife and the open door. They considered each other carefully.

"Better put down the knife," Steve ordered.

The kid took a couple of steps backward, the switchblade at arm's length, ready. He was scared now, and that made him more dangerous. A swaggering, threatening punk had become a cornered animal, jumpy and unpredictable. Steve made a move toward him. The boy lunged.

"Watch out!" Mrs. Rothberg cried.

Steve put his hands on the counter, swung his body up into the air and kicked. Without really thinking about it, he was copying one of the moves in the Captain Avenger television commercial he had seen earlier in the day. It worked. The kid fell back, and the knife went flying.

Before Steve could figure his next move, the boy spotted the switchblade and went for it. Mrs. Rothberg dashed out from behind the counter and kicked the weapon across the floor, toward Steve.

"Son of a bitch!" the kid shrieked. Desperate to get away, he lowered his head and charged. Instead of meeting the attack, Steve took a quick step to the side, caught the boy by the back of his neck and the seat of his pants and propelled him toward the open door. The boy stumbled and almost fell but managed to stay on his feet and kept going, out the door and down the street. A couple of passersby watched wonderingly.

For a moment there was absolute quiet. Then Manny Rothberg broke into a smile. "I don't believe it. If I didn't see it with my own eyes—"

Steve shrugged awkwardly. He didn't believe it either.

"Wait till I tell Sheldon," the old man went on. "He used to read all your comic books."

His wife nodded agreement. "You and Batman."

Rothberg shot her a look. "Captain Avenger was his favorite."

The people on the sidewalk were staring in at Steve as if he were some visitor from outer space.

He looked down at his costume, uncomfortable. "I'd better go now."

Rothberg came out from behind the counter. "Can I get you something?"

Steve shook his head and started to the door.

"Milk," Mrs. Rothberg remembered, hurrying back to the refrigerator.

"I've got some champagne in back," Rothberg offered. "Special."

"No, thanks." Steve was anxious to go.

Mrs. Rothberg came back with a carton of milk and Steve's trench coat. "Yours?" she asked.

"Oh. Yeah. Thanks."

Steve took the milk and the coat, and dug in a pocket for some money. Rothberg put up his hands.

"Please. It's on the house."

Steve smiled and turned to the door. The people standing outside stepped out of his way. He walked quickly off into the night.

Half a block away, alone, Steve stopped to reflect on what he had just done. He leaned against a lamppost and laughed aloud, high on what he did. Then he straightened, suddenly sober. "I could've been killed."

He pulled his coat close around him and walked on.

He was still dazed when he got to his apartment. He took off his coat and sat on the bed, went over the whole episode again in his mind and shook his head incredulously. He started to pull off his boots, caught his reflection in a mirror mounted on the closet door, stood, put his hands on his hips and considered his Captain Avenger image.

"Mind if I drop in?" he asked cockily. Then he grinned. "What a performance!"

He found the telephone cord and followed it until he came to the phone, under some clothes on the bed. He took up the receiver and dialed.

"Hey, Jerry. This is Steve. Are you busy? What kind of party?" He shrugged. "Yeah, I know I could probably pick up something there, but— I don't know, I don't feel like a party. I just wanted to talk. Listen, you won't believe what happened to me. I was on the way home—What? Oh, sure. I can tell you about it another time. Have a good evening."

He clicked off, feeling letdown. Then he dialed again. On the third ring, an answering machine picked up the call:

"This is Marty Fields. You wanna know if you got a job? The answer's no. When it's yes, *I'll* call *you*. Any other business, leave your name and number when you hear the beep."

Steve looked unhappily at the receiver and started to hang up. Then a mischievous gleam came to his eye.

"This is Robert Redford," he said after the beep. "I'm looking for new representation. Sorry you weren't in."

He hung up, smiling, then sighed and put the phone on a bedside table. There had to be somebody— He looked toward the hall and got an idea.

Chapter
Four

AT Sardi's, a small orchestra was playing, while people in formal clothes waved from table to table and blew kisses and watched the door for new arrivals. A woman swept in, trailing fox fur. When the crowd applauded, she opened her arms to the room.

"Move in on Sparky," a voice commanded.

A small army of people watched the action from behind lights and camera. Most of them were young, dressed in jeans or cords, drinking coffee from styrofoam cups, smoking cigarettes.

The camera, mounted on a dolly, was pushed toward a table at the center of the room, where a wirehaired terrier sat with all the self-assurance of a star.

"Cue the waiter."

The man directing was Milo Shale. In his late thirties, he wasn't a handsome man feature by feature, but he had a style, an attitude, that made him attractive. He handled himself with absolute confidence, intense and energetic but never frantic. His jeans were tailored. The loafers were Gucci, the sweater cashmere, the watch Cartier and solid gold. Everything about him spoke of success: a guy who has made it.

A waiter approached Sparky's table, holding a tray high in the air.

"Offer Sparky the charlotte russe."

The tray was brought down to the table.

"He looks."

As the pastry was directly under Sparky's nose, he did seem to be giving it some consideration.

"He turns away."

There was no move from Sparky.

"He turns away," Milo repeated firmly.

The dog's trainer pushed forward and knelt just out of camera range. "Look over here, Sparky."

Sparky turned toward the familiar voice.

Milo spoke to the script secretary, who was never far away. "We'll overcrank that turn."

"Good boy," the trainer encouraged his star.

"Okay. He's turned down the charlotte russe." Suddenly, Milo's tone changed. "Jesus! No wonder he turned it down. Look at it. Cut!"

The action stopped. The music stopped. Milo walked over to Sparky's table for a closer look at the pastry.

"*I'd* pick Supo Dog Food over that." He looked around impatiently. "What's happened to the charlotte russe?"

Jolene came out of the small army. "The lights, Milo. It's melted."

"It has to be a beautiful charlotte russe. The most beautiful charlotte russe in the world."

Jolene was unruffled. "We've got a refrigerator full." She called to a prop man to bring another pastry.

Milo looked at his watch and shrugged to his assistant, who spoke to the crowd. "Okay, everybody relax while we bring out another pastry. But stay in your places. We'll go again right away."

The room was immediately loud with conversation, as extras broke character and members of the crew took advantage of the break to check lights, props, makeup.

Jolene considered a rose in front of Sparky and exchanged it for a fresher-looking flower from another, less conspicuous table. Milo, walking toward the orchestra, gave her a pat on the rear as he passed. She didn't seem to notice.

Milo asked the musicians to show him what they were doing and turned to call for playback.

As the music started, Steve entered the set and swept Jolene into a waltz turn. "May I have this dance?"

"Are you crazy?" She glared at him. "What are you doing here?"

"Dancing. I'm on a high."

"Well, come down." She stopped cold, pushing away from him.

"Don't be sore."

"I am working."

"No, you're not," he smiled. "You're on a break."

A buzzer sounded and the assistant director called everybody back to work.

"Goodbye," Jolene said firmly.

"Okay. I'll go. If that's what you want. Because I am a very nice person. One of the nicest people you know."

"I don't know you."

"I'm working on it."

He flashed an appealing grin and walked off. Jolene looked after him in exasperation.

Milo took command again. "We'll pick it up where the waiter offers the charlotte russe."

The waiter stood at Sparky's table with a fresh

pastry. The assistant director called for quiet. The camera rolled.

"Action!" Milo ordered.

Steve stopped by the door and looked back. Once again, the waiter put a pastry under Sparky's nose. Taking his cue like a pro, the dog turned away.

"Bring in the dog food," said Milo.

A second waiter came to Sparky's table with a tray that held a can of Supo Dog Food.

"Sparky looks. He reacts."

The trainer signaled his star. "Speak, Sparky."

Sparky barked emphatically. The second waiter scooped some dog food into a bowl and put it on the table. He looked at the first waiter to declare in a superior way, "It's a matter of taste."

"Good. Very good. Now Sparky eats the dog food."

Sparky just sat there.

"He's not eating the dog food," Milo said darkly.

"Eat, Sparky," the trainer urged.

There was no move from the star. Milo threw up his hands. "We can't do the commercial if he won't eat the Goddam dog food!"

Sparky jumped to the floor, knocking over his chair, and ran to his trainer.

"Shit! Cut it." Milo looked at the trainer. "What's wrong?"

"It upsets him when you yell."

"It upsets *me* when he won't eat the Goddam dog food."

Steve smiled at the confusion and went out.

As the night passed, the street outside Sardi's grew quiet. Then, about 4 A.M., there was a burst of activity. Cast and crew started pouring out of the restaurant. Steve looked up from where he had been sitting with his back against the building, stretched and got to his feet. Jolene came out. She looked tired.

"How about some coffee?" Steve greeted her.

"I don't believe it."

"I'll even spring for a danish."

She frowned quizzically, not knowing what to make of him. "Tell me, why did you come here?"

He gave an easy shrug. "I wanted to be with somebody." His smile was open, ingenuous.

"Don't you have any friends?"

"Not a lot. Do you?"

"Hundreds." Then she smiled too, in spite of herself. "Give or take a few."

Steve was encouraged by the smile. "Come on. We'll have some coffee. We'll talk. Wait till you hear what happened to me tonight."

Jolene shook her head.

"Okay. No coffee. We'll share a cab home."

"I've got a ride."

"Something special, or just a ride?"

Jolene sighed helplessly. "Look—I've got nothing against you personally. You're a guy in condition and I'm the girl down the hall. Why shouldn't you try? But as it happens—"

She stopped short, reminding herself that she didn't owe him any explanations. She didn't owe him anything at all. But he was so open and agreeable, so well-meaning, she couldn't just tell him to get lost.

"We'll have to do some pickups, but I want to see the rushes first."

They both turned as Milo came through the door, followed by his assistant.

"The lab says two o'clock, Milo."

"I'll be sitting there at noon, waiting. Tell them that." He started for his car, a white 450SL parked in the loading zone right in front of the restaurant. He glanced over at Jolene as he went. "Let's go. I'm bushed."

Jolene looked at Steve, then followed Milo to the car. No explanations were necessary.

Steve watched the Mercedes pull away, sagged unhappily and walked off. Halfway down the block, he came upon a bum, staggering drunk. "Hi."

The bum looked blearily at his unexpected companion.

"You'll never guess what happened to me tonight."

The bum belched.

"Gesundheit. It was a crazy thing. Do you know the West Village?"

As they walked off together, Steve began describing his night's adventure.

At 8:30, Steve's alarm rang. He reached to turn it off, but it wasn't where it should have been. He raised his head groggily, dragged himself out of bed and followed the sound. The clock was on the other side of the room, under a sweatshirt. Steve remembered taking it over there to time some exercises. He looked back at the bed, thought about returning to its warmth, but decided against it. He had to go to work early this afternoon and he had some things to do first.

As he crossed to the kitchen, he punched on his TV. He poured a glass of milk, broke an egg into it and added a scoop of high-protein mix. He stirred the concoction lazily and started to drink.

"We've been talking, maybe we should sell the store and move away."

"After thirty-three years."

Steve looked around, curious. The voices on television sounded familiar. He moved out of the kitchen.

"A thing like last night, it gives you hope."

Steve stood in front of the set and stared in amazement. Mr. and Mrs. Rothberg were being interviewed outside of their grocery store. Curious neighbors stood nearby, stealing self-conscious glances at the camera.

"Do you have any idea who it was?" the interviewer asked.

"Captain Avenger," Mr. Rothberg answered firmly. "Believe me, you couldn't miss it."

Mrs. Rothberg nodded and put her hand to her breast. "A big A, right here."

The newsman's tone was polite but patronizing. "Captain Avenger is a character out of comic books. Don't you wonder who it really was?"

"Why wonder? He comes in my store and takes care of a couple of punks that want to cut my throat. Should I ask for a driver's license?"

"He should only live and be well," Mrs. Rothberg added.

Steve broke into a grin, ran to the door, threw it open and dashed into the hall. He went to Jolene's apartment and knocked. "Hey!" he called through the door. "Turn on your TV."

Another door opened and Mrs. Havachek looked out. A woman in her fifties with an exaggerated idea of her own respectability and that of her building, she stared at Steve in shock and deep disapproval. He looked down at himself and grinned sheepishly. He was still wearing the undershorts he slept in. "I got excited," he explained.

"Please. I'm not interested in your personal life."

Steve moved back to his own door. "I'm on TV, Mrs. Havachek. Right now. This minute."

"With no pants?"

"They're *talking* about me."

"I wouldn't doubt it. Tuesday's the fifteenth, Mr. Nichols."

Steve frowned at the nonsequitur.

"That makes your rent two weeks overdue."

"Oh, right. No problem. I've got a residual coming in."

"You want to stay here, pay your rent. Also, don't go in the hall with no pants."

Her nose in the air, she went back into her apartment. Steve shrugged and walked through his open door.

The newsman was alone now, talking directly to camera. "Calls have been coming into our switchboard—people expressing their gratitude. To whom? Who is Captain Avenger, the man behind the mask?"

Steve addressed the set. "It's me! Steve Nichols."

"There is surprisingly little curiosity about that."

Steve frowned quizzically, as the newsman went on.

"He appeared as Captain Avenger. He did what Captain Avenger is supposed to do. Some people have flatly declared they don't *want* to know his true identity."

Steve sat on the edge of his bed, listening with interest.

"Maybe it's not so hard to understand at that. You can tell a child that Santa Claus is on Macy's payroll, and he may believe you—but he won't thank you for the news. Perhaps the real question is not 'Who are you?' but 'What next, Captain Avenger?'"

Steve blinked in surprise, shaken by the thought. "What do you mean, what's next?"

Chapter
Five

EDDIE Pierce climbed the front steps of a brownstone on the East Side. A polished brass plate by the door read "Walter Reeves, Public Relations."

The interior of the brownstone was a sharp contrast to the exterior. Modern furniture was set against stark white walls. There were a few black and white lithographs, some plants, a lot of chrome and glass. Eddie approached one of three secretaries in a large reception area and asked to see the boss.

The secretary looked up from applying polish to nails too long for typing. "He's busy."

"It's important."

"Calvin Donnelly's in there."

"Uh oh."

"Uh huh."

Eddie looked toward the door to Walter's office. "Let me know when it's over."

Walter's office was also relentlessly modern, antiseptically white, almost forbidding. The man who sat behind the uncluttered glass-topped desk that dominated the room was as sleek as his setting. In his thirties, lean, waspish, he wore jeans and a white silk shirt that was open in front to show silver chains. His aviatorstyle glasses were silverframed. The eyes behind them were black and quick. At the moment, they were following Calvin

Donnelly as he moved around the room. An older man, in a conservative suit and tie, he wasn't pacing so much as he was stalking, tense, ready to pounce.

"Eight weeks from Election Day, and look at us."

"A lot can happen in eight weeks," Walter answered coolly.

"It better."

"He hasn't been a bad mayor."

Donnelly shot him a look. "That's a hell of a campaign slogan."

"We've focused on a solid, responsible job over the past four years."

"And the opposition has focused on blackouts and garbage strikes and crime in the streets, and laid it all on *him*."

"The incumbent is always under attack."

Donnelly moved so suddenly to the desk that Walter sat upright, startled.

"They're killing us, Walter." He leaned across the glass top. "We're trailing in all the polls: the Harris poll, the *New York Times* poll, the six o'clock news—"

Walter was quick to recover his poise. "We could shift emphasis from his record to his personality." He smiled. "If he had one."

Donnelly was not amused. "You're the high-priced PR genius. Work it out." He crossed to the door. "I'll expect to hear something by the end of the week."

"You're pushing me, Calvin."

Donnelly looked back. "That's right," he said flatly. "I am."

After Donnelly walked out, Walter fiddled with

a silver letter opener and muttered, "Son of a bitch."

There was a knock on the door and Eddie stuck his head in.

"You free?"

Walter nodded and Eddie came in, followed by Anthony Caselli. Both men were beaming.

"We've got attendance reports from all the theaters," Eddie announced.

"Lines around the block." Anthony grinned.

"Lines, Walter, to see that turkey." Eddie shook his head in amazement.

"People are going nuts. They're calling in—to radio and TV stations, to City Hall—to say they're happy."

"And they're going to see the movie!"

Walter was listening, but he was staring past his two delighted associates, to something at the other end of the room. He rose and walked around his desk.

"A couple of news guys called here," Eddie reported. "I told Linda to stall 'em till we decide what we want to say."

Walter reached the end of the room, where two posters stood against the wall, one for the mayor's reelection and one announcing the arrival of Captain Avenger. He looked from one to the other.

Eddie watched his boss curiously. "So whadaya think?"

Walter turned with a sly smile. "What do I think? I think Captain Avenger has just saved the mayor's ass."

Eddie and Anthony exchanged glances.

"You guys hired those Yo-Yos we sent out to the theaters. Any idea which one it was?"

Anthony was puzzled. "Who says it was one of ours?"

"He had to have an outfit." Eddie was getting onto Walter's train of thought.

"Some Captain Avenger freak could've made his own costume," Anthony argued. "There must be half a million certified crazies in this city."

"In my heart, I know it's one of ours." Walter started back to his desk. "Find out which one."

"How?" Eddie asked. "Call them all in?"

"All sixty-two?" Anthony was still bewildered by the whole idea.

Walter answered with elaborate patience. "If he wanted us to know who he is, we'd have already heard from him. Check them out, quietly. Which one *could* do it, *would* do it?"

He was pleased with himself. Of course, this Captain Avenger thing was just dumb luck. But Walter knew what do with luck. He knew how to take advantage of situations, how to make mountains out of molehills. It was his business.

"When are you taking them out again?" he asked.

"This afternoon. The three o'clock matinee."

"Okay. Let them keep the costumes. Make up some excuse. And get word out that we're missing one."

Anthony frowned wonderingly. "A guy?"

Walter gave him a look. "A costume. Say it was stolen. That will confuse anybody else trying to find out who he is." He sat behind his desk, relaxed and confident. "What we have here, gentlemen, is a golden opportunity. Let us take it firmly by the private parts."

That afternoon, the Captain Avenger bus pulled

to a stop in front of the Bronx Royal. The air-pressure doors opened and Steve Nichols, in full Captain Avenger regalia, started to step out. He hesitated, astonished by what was waiting for him.

A huge crowd was gathered in front of the theater, and sidewalks were filled for half a block on both sides. It wasn't a rowdy crowd, but it was a very enthusiastic one.

"Here he comes!" someone yelled.

Steve raised his arms in greeting. A cheer went up. Two uniformed policemen came forward to make way for him.

As he moved through the crowd to a preselected spot near the box office, Steve was wearing a happy, dazed expression. What he had heard on TV was true. People were responding to what he did in that grocery store last night. It was important to them.

He got to his position and began shaking hands, signing autographs, having a great time.

Half an hour after Steves' arrival, a TV mobile unit pulled up in front of the theater. Gloria Preston got out and surveyed the scene with a coolly cynical eye. She spoke to her cameraman, as he strapped on equipment: "Well, like I always say, When you think you've seen it all, look again." She pushed into the crowd. "Come on, let's get this over with."

Gloria Preston had indeed seen it all, or felt she had. After her marriage went sour, she dusted off a degree in journalism and went looking for work. She got a number of offers, to be a secretary or a receptionist. She turned them down. Finally, she got a job as a newswriter at TV station WNAT. It didn't pay much, but it got her inside. A year later, she was an on-the-spot newscaster. Smart and aggressive, she was always after the story behind the story, not only *what* happened but *why*. Fraud and corruption were her specialities. She had a nose for them. A couple of times she got the station in trouble, when she smelled more than there was to smell. She was worth the trouble.

The Captain Avenger story was off beat for Gloria. She went after villains, not heroes. But somebody had to do it. At least, that's what the station manager said when he asked her to cover it.

A teenage girl bounced forward to kiss Steve on the cheek.

"What was that for?" he asked good-naturedly.

The girl giggled. "Because you're a fox."

Gloria and her cameraman pushed close. "Gloria Preston, WNAT. How about an interview?" Before Steve could answer, she turned to the cameraman. "Got us both? Good. Let's roll it."

Steve looked self-consciously into the camera, as Gloria spoke into a hand mike: "We're here at the Bronx Royal, where a large crowd is gathered to meet, or just catch a glimpse of, Captain Avenger. People in Brooklyn are doing the same thing, and in Queens, all over greater New York." She turned to Steve. "What do you think about all this attention, Captain Avenger?"

"I think it's great."

"It sure sells tickets."

"That's not what I meant."

"Would you like to introduce yourself?"

When Steve hesitated, Gloria looked at him quizzically. "No?" She turned back to camera and suggested facetiously, "Maybe we've stumbled onto something here."

Steve realized he had made a mistake. "My name is Steve Nichols," he said quickly.

"An actor or a model or what?"

"I'm an actor."

"Tell me, Steve, how do you account for this turnout? Are these people here on the chance that you might be *the* Captain Avenger, the grocery store hero?"

Steve considered a moment. "No, I don't think so. I don't think it's got anything to do with me."

"What then?"

"I think it's the idea."

"Idea?"

"Yeah." He searched for the right words. "It's what Captain Avenger stands for, you know? For right, and for justice. He takes up for the little guy. And he wins. People like that. It makes them feel like—like they've got a chance."

Gloria was unprepared for this outburst of idealism. "Well." She gave him a close look, then turned to the camera: "You've just heard from Steve Nichols, one of the sixty-two Captain Avengers making appearances at movie theaters all over New York City, giving his thoughts on what all this means. An idea come to life—out of the comic section onto the front pages—to make us all feel better. It sounds good to *me*. Hooray for Captain Avenger! And Mickey Mouse for president."

Steven frowned at her sarcasm.

"This is Gloria Preston, WNAT, in the Bronx."
When the camera light went off, she looked back
at Steve. "You were fantastic. Never got out of
character and didn't gag once." She cocked her
head curiously. "Tell me, Steve, what do you look
like with your mask off?"

"Like Captain Avenger without his mask."

Gloria laughed, enjoying that. "Okay. See you in
the funny papers."

She went off through the crowd. Steve looked
after her, annoyed, and vaguely disturbed. Then he
turned to greet people who were moving close
again, holding out slips of apper, reaching to shake
his hand.

An hour later, Steve was back in the yellow
bus. Eddie stood by the driver and made an
announcement to his team of Captain Avengers.
The PR firm was going to schedule some more
appearances, he said, but had been asked to hold
off for a few days, as the crowds were too hard to
handle. It might be the end of the week before
things could get properly organized. He would
be in touch. In the meantime, they might as well
keep their costumes.

"In case, the guy is one of *us*," a Captain Avenger
called from the back of the bus.

There were hoots and laughter.

"It's just a practical thing," Eddie told them.

"Bullshit. That guy last night had on a Captain
Avenger suit. *We* had Captain Avenger suits.
He could be sitting in front of you right now."

"You wouldn't want to turn the guy off," another
Captain Avenger chimed in.

"Yeah. Would he go out in his underwear?"

There was more laughter and animated separate conversations started up all over the bus.

"Okay, okay," said Eddie, taking a seat up front. "Just keep the outfits."

Steve heard someone behind him say, very earnestly, "Hey, it *could* be one of us. Fantastic!"

Chapter
Six

IT was late afternoon when Steve approached his apartment building, dressed in jeans and a sport shirt, carrying an overnight bag that contained the Captain Avenger costume.

Jolene came to the building from the opposite direction. "Hello." She gave Steve a smile.

"Hi." He answered absently.

"J. Marsh," she said, surprised by his indifference. "We're neighbors."

Steve stopped to look at her. "Sorry. My head was somewhere else."

He held open the door. She smiled at the gesture, which had become increasingly rare. It suited him.

"About last night—" she began.

"I shouldn't have barged in like that."

"I could have been nicer. I've been a little uptight lately."

"No problem."

They walked along the corridor, in no hurry.

"I knocked on your door this morning," Steve told her.

"Oh?"

"About eight-thirty. I guess you're a sound sleeper."

"I wasn't there."

"At eight-thirty?"

"I spent the night out."

59

"Hey, that *was* a special ride."

Jolene gave him a look, defensive. "With an old friend."

Steve nodded. "By any chance, does that old friend live on East Sitxy-sixth Street?"

"Who are you, J. Edgar Hoover?"

"No, I'm Captain Avenger."

"Oh, right."

Steve stopped at his apartment door. "I guess you heard about that—what happened last night."

"How could I help?" Jolene kept walking.

"What do you think?"

"The world's full of weirdos."

Steve frowned. "That's it? He's a weirdo?"

"Probably stoned out of his mind, sitting around today, trying to figure out how he did it."

"You have a terrific way of looking at things."

She stopped at her door and looked back at him, annoyed, without really knowing why. "I traded my rosecolored glasses for a crash course in martial arts and a funny little fountain pen that shoots tear gas up to five feet."

"I'll keep my distance." Steve unlocked his door and pushed it open.

"Why did you knock this morning?" Jolene asked.

"Huh?" He turned to her. "Oh, I was going to tell you a funny story."

"So tell me."

"I forgot the punch line." He went into his apartment.

Jolene *was* annoyed. Why should he question her attitudes? And what if he did? Why should it bother her? She had plenty of reason to feel the way she did. Each day brought more reason.

60

Didn't he read the newspapers? Probably only the theater section. She shrugged and stepped inside her door, closing it firmly behind her.

That evening, Steve sat on his bed, eating dinner and watching TV. A man-woman newsteam was on the screen.

"Well, Tracy, it's almost seven-thirty. Any reports of a second appearance by Captain Avenger?"

"No, Bob, but calls have continued to come in all day long, people just wanting to say they feel good because of what happened last night."

"I guess we still need heroes."

Steve flipped a defiant look toward the door to the hall, toward Jolene.

"Speaking of heroes," Tracy continued, "here's an up-date on a very young one. Nine-year-old Tommy Andretti, who saved his four-year-old sister from injury, and possibly death, when he pushed her out of the path of a runaway truck—that was on Wednesday of last week—is facing surgery for injuries he sustained in that incident."

Steve put his dinner aside, his full attention on the screen.

"Doctors at St. Vincent's Hospital report Tommy's condition as good," the woman went on, "but it will be major surgery."

"A lot for a nine-year-old to deal with."

"Indeed it is." Tracy looked directly into the camera. "All of you who care about Tommy and the kind of unselfish bravery he demonstrated, keep him in your thoughts tonight."

"That's our news. Good night, Tracy."

"Good night, Bob. And good night, Captain Avenger, wherever you are."

During the next two hours, Steve picked up the apartment, changed the linens on his bed, lugged a week's worth of newspapers to the incinerator and did some hard exercising. It was all a delaying action, to give himself time to change his mind about what he knew in his heart he was going to do.

At ten o'clock, he walked up the wide front steps of St. Vincent's Hospital, his trench coat belted close around him.

He crossed the lobby to the front desk, where several people were trying to get the attention of an overworked receptionist. Without a word, he checked the revolving index of patients' names, saw that T. Andretti was in Room 312 and moved on.

An elevator opened and two nurses stepped out, talking quietly. Steve went in. One of the nurses suddenly frowned and looked back. Her eyes went to the gold boots that showed below Steve's coat, then up to his face. He smiled, as the elevator doors slid shut.

He stepped out of the elevator near the third floor desk, where a nurse was on the telephone. He turned up his coat collar and started to walk past.

"Excuse me," the nurse called after him, "visiting hours are over."

Steve only half turned, keeping his face as hidden as possible. "That's okay. I'm just passing through." He walked off down the hall, checking room numbers.

For a moment, the nurse semed to accept the explanation—it had been delivered in such a reasonable, matter-of-fact way. Then she frowned and spoke into the phone. "I'm sorry, doctor. There's something I have to see about."

She put down the receiver and got out from behind the desk.

As Steve turned a corner and passed Room 308, he heard hurried footsteps behind him and ducked into a door marked "Men." The nurse came around the same corner and stopped, her features pinched in consternation.

An orderly came out of a ward at the end of the corridor, rolling a utility table.

"Howard, I think there's someone on the floor. Would you please check, while I get back to Dr. Player?"

"Sure."

"Try the men's room."

She walked back to her desk, as the orderly went to the men's-room door.

Howard looked around, pushed open stall doors. No one was there. But on the back of a door, on a metal hook, there was a trench coat. He took it out with him.

Steve was standing on a ledge at the side of a men's-room window. He looked down and, shaken, snapped his head back to the wall. The third floor is a long way up when you're out on a narrow ledge and there's concrete below. He turned to look along the side of the building at a line of windows some ten feet apart. Realizing that Tommy Andretti was only a couple of windows away, he started to move along the ledge, slowly, carefully, hugging the wall.

He came to a window, paused, tried to see in but couldn't. He took a deep breath and started to sidestep across.

A boy, maybe six years old, looked up from his pillow, wide-eyed, as a blue and crimson figure, seen only from the shoulders to the knees, moved across the window. He climbed out of bed, padded over to the window and tapped.

Startled, Steve almost fell. Then, collecting himself, he bent down to look. Behind the glass, a bright, inquisitive face was upturned. "Captain Avenger?" he mouthed. Steve nodded. The boy started to raise the window, but Steve shook his head and put a finger to his lips. The boy nodded and watched Steve move on, pressing his cheek eagerly against the glass.

At the floor desk, the nurse, the orderly and a security guard were talking. The guard was looking at Steve's trench coat. "It wasn't anybody you've seen before."

"I don't think so," the nurse told him. "But I didn't get a very good look."

"I'll make a room-to-room search."

The window of Tommy Andretti's room was a quarter open. Steve pushed it higher and put one leg over the sill. Tommy turned in his bed.

"Hi, Tommy."

The boy just stared, as Steve came into the room and crossed to the bed.

"I know it's after visiting hours, but I couldn't get here any earlier."

"Were you catching crooks?"

"Well, I didn't catch any today. But I'm always on the lookout."

"I heard about you on TV, how you're a real hero and not just made up."

"That's how I heard about *you*."

In the corridor, the nurse and the guard turned

a corner and stopped short. The boy who saw Captain Avenger at his window and three other children were crowded together at the door to Tommy's room.

In the room, Steve and Tommy were still talking.

"You've got a lot of friends out there," Steve affirmed. "That's one good thing about being a hero. People you don't even know really care about you!"

Tommy thought about that. Steve's eyes shifted to the door, where he saw the nurse and the guard standing behind the cluster of children. "Listen, I have to go now. After your operation, when you're feeling good again, maybe we can get together. Okay?"

Tommy nodded firmly. "Okay."

Steve reached for Tommy's hand and they shook in the blood-brothers way. Then he turned from the bed. The kids at the door greeted him with broad smiles.

"Hiya, guys."

"Hi, Captain Avenger."

Steve looked at the nurse and the guard.

"I guess this is yours." The guard handed over the folded trench coat.

"Thanks."

The nurse looked at the children around her, at the excitement and pleasure in their faces, and then back at Steve. "I don't suppose you'd have time to say hello to some others."

"It's up to you."

A dozen kids looked up in astonishment when Captain Avenger walked boldly into their ward.

"Hey, I've got a question."

Eyes and smiles were big, as Steve looked from bed to bed.

"Who says nice guys finish last?"

A black boy near the door sat up straight and called out, "Nobody!"

Steve threw him a salute and eleven others echoed enthusiastically, "Nobody!"

Chapter
Seven

CALVIN Donnelly came out of City Hall, giving instructions on the move to a harried assistant. "You tell him I want what I want when I want it," he growled. "Remind him I'll be around no matter who wins the election. I'll *always* be around."

The assistant nodded and scratched an entry in a notebook as Walter Reeves approached from the street.

"That's all." Donnelly waved the assistant away and looked at Walter. "You're late."

"I'm sorry."

"So am I." He kept walking. "You're out, Walter."

"What?" Walter stopped dead in his tracks, then turned and hurried after the older man.

"We fell another four points in the latest poll." Donnelly thrust a newspaper at Walter.

"I saw that."

"I've been talking with an aggressive young man who's got some bright ideas. He's hungry. That makes people bright."

They reached a waiting limousine. Donnelly's driver was there to open the door.

"Can he bring you the election in a box, gift-wrapped?" Walter asked cockily. "Can he do that, Calvin?"

Donnelly stopped to look at him. "What the hell are you talking about?"

Walter handed back the newspaper. The front page told of Captain Avenger's hospital visit. "That's what I'm talking about. Captain Avenger."

Donnelly frowned wonderingly.

"How do you like what he's doing? How would you like him to keep it up?"

"What's the point?" Donnelly took a cigar out of a silver case. He made no gesture of offering one to Walter.

"The point is, when the people feel good about the city, they feel good about the administration. They're feeling good about the city today. Because of *him*."

"A comic-book hero."

"Read the papers. Watch the news. New York loves Captain Avenger." He smiled. "How would you like him to stay in action right up to Election Day?"

"You can promise that?" Donnelly tried to mute his excitement. He had to play a close hand. "You can tell him what to do and when to do it?"

"I set up the whole thing in the first place. I turned a third-rate movie into the biggest hit of the year, with a simple gimmick: 'Captain Avenger comes to your neighborhood.'"

"Who is he?"

Walter shook his head. "Uh uh."

Donnelly considered a moment. "There would have to be a closer connection."

"Of course." Walter was way ahead of him. "Photographs for the media: Captain Avenger meets the mayor. Two crusaders working together toward a common goal, a better life for the people of New York City."

"He should do some bigger stuff, with more witnesses."

"In the planning stages."

Donnelly started to smile. "I was selling you short, Walter." He opened the silver case, held it out.

"No, thanks." Walter was feeling his power. "I'll tell you what I want."

Donnelly's smile faded.

"I want the city, as a client."

"There are long-standing commitments, outside my influence."

"Extend your influence."

They looked at each other for a long moment. Suddenly they were both smiling. The bargain was struck.

"Now I'll take that cigar," said Walter.

Steve walked out on a bare stage. The stage manager announced, "This is Steve Nichols."

A voice came out of the darkened theater. "Hello, Steve."

Steve shielded his eyes from the footlights and squinted. He could make out three people sitting several rows back. "Hi." He smiled, trying to cover his nervousness.

"How are your impersonations?"

Steve was thrown by the question. "Impersonations? Uh—who do you want?"

"Do C. Aubrey Smith."

Steve frowned quizzically. He couldn't be hearing right.

"You don't know C. Aubrey Smith?"

"Well, yeah, from old movies. That's a tough one."

"Give it a whirl."

Steve considered a moment, started to speak. Nothing came out. "I must have left my impersonations in my other pants," he smiled.

"You came down here to audition, didn't you?" The voice had an edge to it now.

"Yeah, sure."

"This is it."

Steve shifted his weight from one foot to the other, trying desperately to think of some way to handle the situation. He didn't want to give up this chance at a Broadway show. "I can do Clark Gable," he offered. Without waiting for a reply, he threw himself into it. 'I don't know about tomorrow, but tonight you're the most beautiful woman in the world. Does that mean anything to you?'"

There was a long silence. Then the voice said, "Thank you."

Steve nodded and walked off.

A few minutes later he was sitting at the bar in Joe Allen's. The place was quiet at midafternoon, nearly empty. He ordered a beer and thought about what had just happened to him. C. Aubrey Smith. Jesus! A chance, finally, to audition for a part in a play and the director had to be some kind of sadist!

"A passing motorist reported seeing Captain Avenger outside the bank, routing as many as five men with nothing but his bare fists."

Steve looked up at a TV set mounted at the end of the bar, as a commentator continued:

"A police spokesman has acknowledged that a break-in attempt was made at the Brooklyn bank last night but had no comment on what, or who, thwarted the effort."

Steve shook his head, incredulous. People were starting to see things!

"Did you read in the paper? That woman in Queens? He saved her from being raped."

Steve shifted his attention to two attractive young women sitting farther down the bar.

"After, he carried her back to her apartment."

"Carried her? Captain Avenger carried her?"

The first young woman sighed. "Wouldn't you die?"

Her friend made a gesture of exaggerated rapture. She turned her head and her eyes fell on Steve.

He offered her one of his best Captain Avenger smiles.

"Do you mind?" the young woman said, annoyed.

Steve walked along Grove Street, dejected, reflecting on the irony of things. Captain Avenger was a success without trying, getting credit for things he didn't do. Steve Nichols knocked himself out and got nowhere. What would people say if he told them they were one and the same, the superhero and the out-of-work actor who couldn't do C. Aubrey Smith? They wouldn't believe it. Steve could hardly believe it himself. His mind rambling this way, he turned into number twenty-six.

He stopped to get mail from his box. There was nothing of interest. As he walked on to his apartment, a door opened and Mrs. Havachek stepped out. "Hello, Mrs. Havachek," he said with forced good cheer. "How are you this evening?"

"I'd be better if I had the rent."

"I don't know what happened to my residual. They're running that commercial a lot. Maybe you've seen it." He smiled encouragingly.

"I only watch public broadcasting."

Another door opened. It was Jolene, dressed for an evening out.

"Hello." She was a little bit guarded, remembering their last encounter. "I haven't seen you in a while."

"You look great." It was the purest kind of appreciation.

"Thanks." She was disarmed. "How's the acting business?"

"Touch and go."

She smiled, then walked off down the hall. Mrs. Havachek watched Steve watching Jolene.

"Tonight, Mr. Nichols."

Steve looked back at the landlady, dug in his pocket and counted out what he found there. "$10.25. You want it?"

Mrs. Havachek stiffened.

"Give me a break." He went into his apartment.

Later that evening, Steve forced himself to work out. He was doing sit-ups on his slantboard when an interview show came on TV. A moderator talked with Dr. Joyce Brothers and newswoman Gloria Preston about the most popular subject of the day.

"New York has gone Captain Avenger crazy. As a psychologist, Dr. Brothers, do you consider that a good or a bad thing, healthy or unhealthy?"

"Your question is not as simple as it sounds. On

the one hand, who will say it's unhealthy to admire this kind of hero figure?"

"I will," Gloria interrupted.

Steve's sit-ups continued without losing a beat, but as he came up, he turned his head toward the screen.

"Next we'll be looking for genies in bottles and expecting our fairy godmothers to take us to the ball."

The moderator responded to her cynicism. "But Gloria, there *is* someone out there."

"Who? Captain Avenger is fiction. There aren't any heroes anymore."

"Yet, the response to Captain Avenger indicates people are ready for one," Dr. Brothers smiled.

Steve counted his last sit-up and lay back for a moment, breathless.

"All right," Gloria answered. "And tell me what happens when they find out it's a joke or a con?"

"Maybe they won't. Maybe it's not. Inside that costume, there's a real person, with the capacity to be heroic."

Steve got up, checked the clock on the bedside table and went to the closet, pulling off his sweatshirt. Dropping it on the floor, he went quickly through his clothes. He pulled a leather jacket off a hanger, took a cabbie's hat off the shelf, then bent down to pick up a pair of scuffed shoes.

"Doesn't that lead us to another concern?" the moderator was saying. "Even if we assume his sincerity, don't we have to ask ourselves, how far will he go? How far *can* he go? Maybe it's inevitable that he will finally let us down."

"He can't let us down if we don't let him send us up," Gloria offered.

Dr. Brothers was quick to respond. "You're saying give up hope. I never recommend it. People need their hopes, just as they need their fantasies. We are still dreamers, after all."

Steve's eyes shifted to something else, at the back of the closet—a pair of gold boots.

Chapter
Eight

STEVE sat in his cab at a traffic signal. It was a dreary night, a light rain falling. When the light changed, he shifted into first. The engine died. He sighed, turned the ignition key and pumped the accelerator with a gold boot. When the engine caught, he checked traffic and pulled away, reaching to turn on a portable radio that sat on the seat beside him. Equipped with a scanner, the radio was bringing in police calls. Steve drove slowly, listening, watching both sides of the street. There weren't many people out. A couple ran down the sidewalk, sharing an umbrella. For a while, the calls on the radio were routine. Then: "Nine L Twenty-one in pursuit of a black sedan, headed east on Tenth Street at Broadway."

Steve, reacting to the call, stopped at an intersection, rolled down his window and looked out at the street signs. "Second Avenue and Fourth Street," he said aloud.

A man with a newspaper over his head ran up to the cab. Steve looked at him, made a quick decision and hit the accelerator. As the cab leaped away, the man yelled obscenities.

Steve peered past the blur of windshield wipers, as the voice on the radio fed him more information: "Black sedan, license 287 FDH, on Tenth, approaching Second Avenue."

Steve swung the cab into Tenth Street and was passed by a speeding car. The license number was 287 FDH. A flashing red light was behind him, caught in traffic. He was in the middle of the chase.

The sedan and the cab raced along, changing lanes back and forth to miss other vehicles. Suddenly a car started out of a cross street. Its driver, seeing the oncoming sedan, panicked and stopped in the middle of the intersection. An approaching car kept the sedan from swerving out. It slowed, giving Steve a chance to catch up. When the sedan pulled out, speeding up again, the cab was there to cut it off, forcing it into a lamppost. Two men jumped out, one of them carrying a suitcase.

The door of the cab was thrown open and Captain Avenger appeared.

The two men stopped to stare at Steve in disbelief, then jerked their heads around at the sound of a siren. "This way." The man with the suitcase tapped his partner on the shoulder and nodded toward the side street. They started to go.

"Hold it!" Steve came forward.

Without hesitation, one of the men pulled a revolver.

Steve blinked in surprise. It was the last thing he expected. He twisted around, looking for cover. The gun exploded. Steve fell and the two men took off.

A squad car approached, siren screaming, lights flashing, and swung into the side street.

Steve crawled out of shadows, clutching his right arm. A darker red was starting to show through the ripped sleeve of his costume. With effort, he got into the driver's seat and pulled the door shut.

The cab drove off, weaving at first, then straightening, like a drunk getting control.

At 26 Grove Street, Steve stumbled down the dim hall to his apartment. His mask was off. His jacket was thrown over his shoulder, only his good arm in its sleeve. He carried his change holder and his cabbie's I.D. He leaned against his door and dug in his pocket for keys. Then he looked up and stared in surprise. There was a padlock on the door.

"Oh, no. Oh, shit." He put his forehead against the door and sank slowly to his knees. "Shit—shit—shit."

He fell to one side and sat slumped against the door. His face was white and beaded with perspiration. He started to shiver. When the front door opened, he looked anxiously in that direction, but he didn't have the strength to move.

Jolene came down the hall, headed for her apartment. She stopped to frown curiously. "S. Nichols? Is that you?"

Steve looked up at her but didn't say anything. The fact was, he didn't know what to say.

She moved closer. "Drunk as a skunk." She started to laugh. Then she saw his bloody sleeve and pulled back, frightened.

"Don't call anybody."

"But your arm—" She reached down to him. "I'll help get you inside."

"It's locked."

"What?" She looked up and saw the padlock.

"I didn't pay the rent."

"Ah, Mrs. Havachek, you're a wonderful person." She looked back at Steve and suddenly the costume registered. "What have you got on?" she asked, her eyes covering the outfit. "It's a gag, right? You've been to a costume party."

"No."

"Then *what?* You're not going to tell me that S. Nichols is—" She couldn't say it.

Steve nodded. "Captain Avenger."

"I don't believe it."

"It's true." He smiled in a vaguely embarrassed way.

Jolene stared at him for a long moment, trying to assimilate this incredible thing, trying to decide how she should deal with it. When Steve winced and closed his eyes, her attention went back to the wounded arm.

"Have you got a bullet in there?"

Steve shook his head.

"But you were shot."

He nodded.

"Well, you can't just lie here." She made a decision. "I'd better get you into my apartment. Can you stand up?"

"I think so." He leaned back against the door and pushed himself up to a standing position.

Jolene put her shoulder under his good arm and helped him down the hall. "You don't *look* this heavy," she remarked, staggering under his weight.

"I'm sorry you have to deal with this."

"You and me both."

"I don't think it's too bad. It's stopped bleeding."

"Don't talk. Especially about bleeding. I have a problem with that."

Still supporting him, she stopped at her door and fumbled with the lock. Steve turned his head slightly, putting his face into her hair. It was soft as silk and smelled wonderful.

Jolene finally got the door open and they crossed to her bed, with only the light from the hall to show the way.

"Do you have a doctor?"

"Yeah." He smiled weakly. "Only he's back in Cawker City."

"That's where you're from?"

"Uh huh."

"Figures." She lowered him onto the bed with a sigh of relief, then turned to the phone. "I'll call Emergency."

"No!"

She gave him a quizzical look.

"They report gunshot wounds. It'll ruin everything. Please."

Jolene couldn't believe what was happening. Of all the beds, in all the apartments, in all of New York City, Captain Avenger had to end up in hers. And she was cooperating! She was protecting him, keeping his secret. *Why?* It would be so much easier to pick up the phone and let him be somebody else's problem. That arm of his should get some kind of attention.

"I'll be all right." He looked into her face, read her mind. "Honest. If I can just rest here for a while."

She gestured helplessly. "Okay. I don't know which one of us is crazier, but okay."

Steve sighed and closed his eyes. The bed did feel good. He finally let himself relax, and the whole crazy night drifted away.

Chapter
Nine

STEVE woke slowly, looked around with a confused frown, tried to raise himself on his elbows, but winced and had to take the weight off his wounded arm. He lay back for a moment and let last night's events fall into place. "J. Marsh?" He turned his head to the room.

There was no response. A pillow and a blanket on the sofa indicated someone had slept there. Steve took a deep breath and sat on the edge of the bed. His eyes made a slow tour of the place.

Jolene's apartment was just like his own. That is, it was the same space, laid out in the same way. But what a difference. The walls were freshly painted a soft pastel color, the old moldings just a shade darker for contrast. All the upholstered furniture was covered in the same bright print. There were art posters on the walls, and plants everywhere.

Steve smiled. Here he was, in the beautiful apartment of the beautiful girl down the hall. True, he had to get shot to do it. He looked at his arm. Only a flesh wound, he thought, remembering the standard line from old movies. Actually, that's just what it was. Nothing serious. But it did sting, and his arm was a little stiff.

He looked again at the sofa and wondered where

Jolene had gone. He stood, took a moment to get steady on his feet, then crossed to the bathroom.

Jolene stopped just inside the door, surprised to see the bed unoccupied, then heard water running and came farther into the apartment. "What are you doing?" she asked.

Steve turned from the sink, his mouth full of foam. "Brushing my teeth." He was using his forefinger as the brush. "Also fighting tooth decay."

"A hero's work is never done. Get back in bed."

He looked at her.

"Get back in bed," she repeated firmly.

Steve rinsed out his mouth and went to lie down, wondering what she had in mind.

"Are you hungry?"

"No."

"Good. Then we can get this over with." She sat on the edge of the bed, close to him. She was carrying a paper bag and a newspaper.

"Get what over with?"

"This nice man at the pharmacy told me what to do."

Steve frowned anxiously.

"Don't worry. I told him my dog had an accident."

"With a gun?"

"He didn't know it was loaded. After all, he's only a dog."

They exchanged a quick smile. Then Jolene was all business. She emptied out the bag. There was antiseptic, cotton pads, salve, adhesive tape. She opened a drawer in a bedside table and produced some scissors. "It's only fair to warn you," she said, scissors poised, "that I am not experienced at this sort of thing and may faint."

Steve watched as she carefully cut open the sleeve of his costume. "I don't expect you to take care of me."

"Who do you suggest?"

The wound was in the open now. Jolene wet a pad with antiseptic, braced herself and started cleaning the area. Steve kept watching her, responsive to her nearness, enjoying the attention.

"Did you pick this up in the vicinity of Tenth Street and Avenue C?"

Steve frowned curiously. "How did you know?"

"The guy that shot you wants credit. But since nobody saw you, he's having a hard time." She reached for the newspaper. "I picked this up in case you keep a scrapbook."

Steve opened the paper and started to read a front page news report. "A quarter-million dollars worth of angel dust?" He was stunned.

"Hardly a record. But after all, it was your first bust."

"Ouch!" Steve jumped when she touched the wound itself.

"Try not to cry out. This is touch and go for me."

"Sorry."

Jolene looked at him wonderingly. "You really didn't know what you were getting into last night?"

Steve shook his head, still reading.

"Who sends you out on these missions, your agent?"

"No, he only sends me on beer commercials."

They both smiled. Then Jolene turned away, vaguely uncomfortable, opened a tube and spread some salve on a pad of cotton gauze. "Why?" she asked. "*Why* do you do it?"

Steve considered a moment before answering. "Because of what happened. All those people calling in and writing letters. How often do you get to do something really special?" He found her eyes. "You know what I mean?"

Jolene studied him thoughtfully. "You're for real, aren't you? Honest to God."

Steve gave an almost apologetic shrug.

"And nobody knows."

"Just you."

Uncomfortable again, she got very busy taping the gauze to his arm. "So what do you do, keep it up till somebody kills you?"

"No. If they're gonna use real bullets, I think I'll retire."

In the street, a horn sounded three times.

"That's for me." She quickly finished the bandaging.

"You're going out." He was surprised, and disappointed. Wasn't she going to stay here and take care of him?

"I've got a date."

"Mr. Mercedes?"

"His name is Milo." She moved away, crossed the room to a dressing table and checked her makeup.

There was another honk. Steve looked toward the window. "I'm in your way," he shrugged. "I'll get out of here."

"Where will you go?" Jolene looked at him in the mirror. "And of course, you're in great shape to travel."

"I could manage." Steve sat up, as if to demonstrate his ability to function. "If I had something to put on—"

"Can you wear a size seven in junior dresses?" Her eyes covered his chest and shoulders. "No, I guess not."

Sitting there on the bed, offering to go but not really wanting to, Steve looked like a lost kid or a homeless puppy. Vulnerable. Totally harmless. And very appealing.

"Listen, it's all right if you stay here until you're better." She looked away from him. "You don't take up much room and I'm gone a lot."

Steve stared at her, surprised. She was tossing things into a catchall bag, avoiding his eyes.

"I don't even know your name. What the *J* stands for."

"Jolene." There was a certain challenge in the way she said it.

"Oh." He took a moment. "That's nice."

She gave him a sideways glance. He had a straight face.

"Listen, J, I'll tell you what I'll do."

She smiled, enjoying the way he handled it.

"I'll move to the sofa."

"Thanks," she nodded. "I accept."

After she went out, Steve lay back on the bed with a pleased expression. It was nice here. And J would be back.

It was after midnight when Jolene quietly turned her key in the lock. A light had been left on in the bathroom, so the apartment was not totally dark. She crossed to the closet and started to get out of her clothes.

"Hi."

She turned, startled. Steve was lying on the sofa, his good arm folded behind him.

"It's just me, Captain Avenger."

"I thought you'd be asleep."

She continued to undress, staying behind the closet door.

"That was a long date."

"We lingered over dinner."

"Where'd he take you? Elaine's?" Steve couldn't help being sarcastic. He was jealous.

"We went to a little restaurant in Chinatown."

"Ahh—Oriental atmosphere curiously seductive." Steve's accent was out of old movies.

"I like Chinese food," Jolene said flatly.

"Gentleman strive to please. He want you back in house on Sixty-six Street."

"Confucius say grandma have long nose."

Steve dropped the accent. "I care about these things now that I'm living with you."

"You're not living with me."

"Visiting you."

In a nightgown now, Jolene passed Steve on her way to the bathroom. "Yes, he wants me back."

"What about you? How do *you* feel about it?"

"Excuse me, but that's none of your business." She turned on the tap and started washing her face.

Steve raised his voice. "Well, don't let him rush you. A guy like that can be very pushy."

"And how do you know that?"

"The car. It's a dead giveaway."

"You're crazy. Of course, that's not exactly a news flash."

Jolene turned off the water and flipped the light switch, then crossed in darkness to her bed. Steve sniffed her perfume, heard her slide between sheets. "Steve," he said quietly. "*My* name is Steve."

When she answered, her voice was soft. "Good night, Steve."

"Good night, J"

They both felt it, that somehow across the darkened room, they had touched.

Chapter
Ten

IN Walter Reeves's office, Eddie and Anthony presented the results of their search for a hero.

"Jeff Goldstein." Anthony handed over an eight-by-ten glossy.

Walter gave him an impatient look. "A Jewish Captain Avenger?"

"Why not?"

"Captain Avenger is a WASP."

"Maybe he doesn't know that. Everything else is good. He's an acrobat, an amateur boxer, lives in the Village—"

Walter tossed the photo aside.

"This is Steve Nichols." Eddie offered an actor's composite. "He does gymnastics at the Y. The coach there says he's in good shape."

Walter considered the candidate.

"I was with him that first day," Eddie continued.

"And?"

"He's sort of—strange."

"He's not a pansy, is he? I won't go with a pansy."

"No, not that. He took the Captain Avenger thing very seriously, really played the part, wanted kids to like him."

Walter stared at the composite for another moment, then turned to the next submission.

"That's Roger Terry," Anthony told him. "Actor, model, into body building."

"That's it," said Eddie. "Six guys. You want to see 'em all?"

Walter took another quick look at the possibilities. "No, just this one." He pointed. "I've got a feeling, this is our guy."

Jolene looked up from a magazine and tried not to laugh. Steve had come out of the bathroom in a pink nylon robe that hit him mid-calf, sleeves almost at the elbows, a hairy chest in the cleavage. "At home with Captain Avenger," she observed.

"Where are my pants?"

"Still soaking. Fighting crime is a dirty business."

Steve smiled self-consciously and went to sit on the bed.

"Did you have a nice bath?"

"Yes, thank you." He was having some trouble with the skirt of the robe, which wasn't cut full enough for his frame.

Jolene watched, amused. "Didn't your mother ever tell you to cross your legs?"

Steve, playing modesty, put a pillow in his lap. They both laughed.

"I guess you're feeling better."

"In the pink."

Jolene reacted to the pun, then looked back at her magazine. "I suppose I could talk to Mrs. Havachek, make up some sob story and see if she'd let you back in your apartment." The suggestion was made in the most offhand way.

"I suppose you could." Steve tried to sound casual about it too. "Of course, my residual might come today. And that would take care of everything."

"Maybe we should wait for the mail." Jolene flipped pages.

"Might as well."

They were both willing to delay the issue. The fact was, they were enjoying each other's company. A knock on the door startled both of them.

"Expecting somebody?" Steve asked.

Jolene shook her head.

"I'll make myself scarce."

Steve went back to the bathroom. Jolene crossed to the door and opened it. Milo came in without an invitation. "Get your toothbrush," he ordered. "We're going sailing."

"We're *what?*" Jolene glanced nervously toward the bathroom.

"Mr. Supo Dog Food wants to take me out on his forty-footer. He said to bring along the playmate of my choice. That's you."

"Thanks. But I've got plans."

Milo frowned. "What kind of plans?"

"Personal plans."

Milo moved closed to her. "Hey, didn't we come to an agreement last night?"

"Not that I remember." She took a step back. Milo was an attractive man, a very physical man. When he wanted his way with Jolene, he started touching. It had worked a lot of times. She didn't want that happening now.

"Sure we did." He advanced again, slipped his arms around her.

In the bathroom, Steve had his ear pressed against the door. For several reasons, he didn't like the idea of Mr. Mercedes being in the apartment.

"You came to an agreement with yourself," Jolene declared firmly, as she extracted herself from Milo's embrace.

"We'll talk about it later. I paid a kid to watch my car. I figure if I'm gone more than ten minutes, he'll strip it himself."

Jolene resented the way he brushed her objections aside. "Milo, you can be very pushy!"

Steve smiled at that.

"All right, we'll talk about it *now*." He tried to move in on her again.

"No." She resisted his advance. "I'm getting angry, Milo."

"Why? Because I want to stop you from making a very large mistake?"

Jolene looked at him, annoyed. He was so goddam confident. That had appealed to her once. It didn't appeal to her anymore. In fact, she was amazed at how unappealing it had become.

"We belong together," he said smoothly. "We're a team."

"Not true. I'm a part of *your* team."

"Haven't I taken good care of you?"

"You treat me like a thing. I hate being a thing."

"We'll work it out." He was being tolerant. "Come on, let me take you out of this hole."

"This hole happens to be my home!" she exploded. "And I want you out of it."

"Hey, take it easy—"

"Now, Milo." She moved toward the door.

Milo didn't like being pushed around. He was a pusher. "I'll go when I'm good and goddam ready," he declared.

The door to the bathroom opened and Steve

stepped out. Even in the pink robe, he cut an impressive figure.

"I'm counting to three, Milo."

"Who the crap it *that?*"

"One."

"You'd better go," Jolene suggested quietly.

"Two."

"Nobody makes an ass out of me!" Milo said firmly.

Steve made a menacing move forward. Whereupon, Milo turned and left. Jolene closed the door, leaned against it and started to cry.

"Hey, that was good riddance." Steve walked over to her. "He's not the guy for you. I knew that the first time I saw him."

Jolene whirled on him. "You don't know anything! A crazy man who dresses up in a comic-book suit and goes out doing good deeds, like some overgrown boy scout!"

"I'd never treat you like a thing," he said softly.

She looked at him, tears rolling down her face, and suddenly she was in his arms.

"Who are you?" she asked helplessly. "And what are you doing in my apartment?"

"You want me to leave?"

"Yes."

He started to go.

"No."

She pulled him back, grabbing his wounded arm.

"Ouch!"

"I'm sorry."

"That's okay."

They looked at each other, and slowly their faces came together. They kissed warmly, tenderly.

"I don't want to get involved," Jolene protested. "I just got *uninvolved*."

Steve nodded, but he kept kissing her neck and nuzzling her ear.

"A struggling actor from Cawker City, and a nut at that. A nice nut. But a nut's a nut. I don't need it—"

They kissed again, and Jolene gave in to the nut from Cawker City. He had relaxed and charmed her. He had caught her with her defenses down. It felt good to give in.

Two hours later, Jolene was dressed to go out, limping around the apartment on one shoe. Steve was sitting up in bed, looking very contented. "I want you to know, I'm not always this easy," he grinned.

"I'll bet you say that to all the girls." She looked around, frustrated. "I don't suppose you've seen a black mid-heel pump?"

"Do you have to go?"

"Job interviews are very important at this point, since I don't think I'll be doing much work for Milo."

"Don't worry, I'll take care of you."

"I don't want to be taken care of." She got down on hands and knees to look under the bed. "And you can't take care of *yourself*."

"My luck is changing."

"You're sure about that."

"Yep. Yours too."

"Maybe you're right. I found my shoe." She pulled out the errant pump and sat on the sofa to put it on.

"What brought you to New York?"

"A bus."

When Steve gave her a look, she smiled and offered a straight answer. "I saw myself on the cover of *Vogue*."

"You're pretty enough."

"That's what they said back in Texas. I was Miss Sweetwater and college homecoming queen. Do you know how many homecoming queens there are in New York?" She stood and straightened her skirt, then crossed to a mirror to check herself.

The memory of those first months in the city was all too fresh—modeling swimsuits during Buyers Week and losing the job halfway through because she bruised easily, literally walking the streets to look for work because she couldn't afford taxis.

"When did you decide to get a job behind the camera?"

"When I couldn't get one in front."

In the mirror, she could see Steve's sympathetic expression. She turned with a smile. "Don't feel sorry for me. I'm wiser without being sadder, and today's today. I take things as they come."

Steve smiled too and crooked his forefinger. "Come here."

"Uh uh."

"Just for a minute."

"I've got to go."

She crossed to the door and opened it. Eddie was standing there, ready to knock.

"Well. Hello." He looked her over appreciatively. "I'm looking for Mr. Steve Nichols."

"His apartment is down the hall."

"But he's not in it. The manager thought you might know where he is."

"I wonder where she gets her ideas."

"I'm from Walter Reeves Public Relations." He held out a business card. "It's important I speak to Mr. Nichols. About a job."

Jolene smiled nicely. "Would you excuse me a second?"

She closed the door and turned to Steve, showing the card.

"That's the people that hired me to do Captain Avenger. Better let him come in."

Jolene nodded and opened the door again. "I've just located him."

She stepped back and Eddie walked into the apartment. Steve greeted him with deliberate good cheer. "Hiya, Eddie. Nice to see you again."

Eddie looked at Steve in bed, then back at Jolene, who was lingering out of curiosity, then back at Steve again. The assumption he made was obvious. And of course it was accurate. His eyes fastened on Steve's bandaged arm. "Hurt yourself?"

"Yeah. I—fell."

"Uh huh. Well, listen, Steve, Mr. Reeves would like to talk to you, about something very interesting."

Steve hesitated. "It might be hard for me to do it today."

"I paid your rent, if that helps."

Steve was taken aback. "Yeah, that does help." He and Jolene exchanged a glance.

"Give me five minutes, okay?"

"Sure." With another look at Jolene, Eddie went back into the hall.

"I told you our luck was changing," Steve smiled.

Jolene smiled too. But there was some poignancy in the moment. They would certainly see each other again, but not under the same circumstances. A very special episode was over.

Steve went to the door. He turned back, wanting to say something, to express his feelings.

"Don't wear pink," Jolene suggested with mock-seriousness.

The joke cut through sentiment. Steve nodded and went out.

Chapter
Eleven

EDDIE ushered Steve into Walter Reeves's sleek inner sanctum. Walter was immediately on his feet, coming forward, smiling. "So this is Steve Nichols." He put out his hand. Steve awkwardly offered his left.

"He had an accident," Eddie explained. He and Walter exchanged a glance. Walter was pleased with that information.

"Nothing serious," Steve shrugged.

"It's a pleasure to meet you." Walter shook Steve's left hand.

"A pleasure meeting *you*, Mr. Reeves."

"Walter," he urged. "Call me Walter." He put his arm around Steve's shoulder and guided him toward a seating arrangement at the end of the room. "Come sit down. I believe this chair is the most comfortable."

Steve sat obligingly in the chosen chair. Walter remained standing, studying him. "Goddamit, Steve, this is a moment."

Steve shifted uncomfortably.

"I'm not going to dick you around," Walter continued. "We know what you've been doing."

Steve's throat went dry. "You do?" he rasped.

"A beautiful thing."

"Beautiful," Eddie agreed.

Steve wasn't going to make it that easy. "I'm not

sure I know what you're talking about," he said
guardedly.

Walter smiled, expecting that. "You can relax
with us, Steve. Kick off your boots, take off your
mask."

It was a moment before Steve said anything.
"How did you find out?"

"A little detective work."

"I knew you were special that first night," Eddie
added. "The Elmwood Theater."

"I was doing a job."

"It was more than that."

"Much more," Walter emphasized. "You had your
heart in it. And that's what we had to look for
when we set out to find Captain Avenger. Not just
brawn or brain, but heart." He gave Steve a few
seconds to absorb it all. Walter was too smart to
rush things.

Steve took a deep breath. "So, what happens
now?"

"We'd like to help you," Walter answered simply.

"To do what?"

"Finish what you started."

"I didn't really start anything."

"He turns the city upside down and says he
didn't start anything."

Walter laughed. So did Eddie.

Then Walter was serious again. "The question
is, how long can you keep it up?"

"I have to quit. I know that."

"That's what we want to talk to you about."
Walter sat on the edge of a coffee table, facing
Steve.

"Quitting?"

"How to do it. You can't just walk away."

"In a few weeks, you'd be forgotten." Eddie shook his head unhappily.

"You want to go out a legend," Walter continued.

Steve looked from one to the other. "It was just something that happened—almost an accident."

"Don't make little of it," Walter admonished. "Not even in modesty. It's too important—the need you've touched, the faith you've restored—I doubt if you realize yourself what you've done, what you still can do." His eyes sparkled with a kind of evangelical verve.

"What it takes is a little planning," Eddie offered. "To go out big."

Steve began to understand what was happening, what all this was leading to. "You mean a setup," he said softly.

"A performance," Eddie corrected.

"I can't do that."

"Why not?" Walter seemed genuinely bewildered by Steve's attitude.

"It's wrong."

"Do you play *Hamlet* with real swords?"

"That's different. A play. It's make-believe."

"What's Captain Avenger?"

The question gave Steve pause.

"We're talking about a fine line here." Walter leaned forward urgently. "You did something beautiful. You played the role of Captain Avenger to do it, wore a costume. Does that make it less beautiful, less honest?"

Steve wrestled with the logic Walter used so smoothly. "I *didn't* fake it," he explained.

"Forgive me, Steve, I think you're being selfish."

"Huh?" He was unprepared for Walter's change of tack.

"You're holding back on something they want." He gestured toward the window. "Those people out there. They want their superhero and all he stands for, to hold onto, to tell their kids about."

"You can't stop now," Eddie added. "You've got their hopes up."

"Give them what they want." Walter put his hand on Steve's arm. "Give them the legend."

Steve was confused. There were too many angles. "Let me think about it, okay?"

"Of course."

Steve was surprised at how easily Walter backed off. Both men stood.

"Tell me something, Mr. Reeves, why do you care about this so much?"

Eddie looked at his boss with a flicker of anxiety. But Walter wasn't thrown. He answered simply, with a modest smile, "Somebody has to care."

Steve nodded, accepting that, and started out. Walter walked him to the door. "Do you know Zev Bufman, Steve?"

"The producer?" There was immediate awe in his voice.

Walter nodded. "We're old friends. He's planning a revival of *Cat On A Hot Tin Roof* and he wants a new face for the part of—what's the character?"

"Brick?"

"I think he ought to talk to you."

"Brick." Steve was stunned. He remembered Paul Newman in the film version.

"I'll mention it to him," Walter promised casually.

"Thanks. Thanks a lot." Steve went out in a daze.

Walter buzzed his secretary. "Get me Calvin Donnelly at City Hall."

"Shouldn't you wait till your hear back from the guy?" Eddie cautioned.

"Don't worry," Walter smiled, "he's hooked."

The door opened again and Steve stuck his head in. "Sorry, Mr. Reeves. I can't do it."

Walter and Eddie stared, dumbfounded.

"I just can't. Thanks anyway."

With an apologetic shrug, he was gone. Walter hit the intercom again. "Nevermind Donnelly. If he calls here, I'm out."

Out on the sidewalk, Steve was in a solemn mood. He had just retired Captain Avenger from service and lost a chance at a fantastic career break, and he didn't feel good about either move. But he *should* feel good. He did the right thing, the honest thing. He didn't sell out. He looked up, smiled and said it aloud—"I did the right thing!" A woman passing by gave him a curious look. He didn't notice. He broke into a run and signaled for a taxi.

He got out of the cab in an area of shops and restaurants near his apartment building, picked up a bouquet of flowers, a bottle of wine and some Chinese food. By the time he got to Twenty-six Grove Street, he was whistling happily.

Mrs. Havachek was sweeping the vestibule.

"Ah, Mrs. Havachek," he sang out cheerfully. "How are you this afternoon?"

She looked at him suspiciously.

"That's good." He breezed past her. "I'm fine too."

He went to Jolene's door and knocked. When she

113

appeared in the pink robe, he smiled. "It looks better on you."

Jolene looked at his armload. "What's all this?"

"Dinner. The old Chinese seducation. Oh, and flowers for the lady of the house."

He held out the bouquet, which she accepted with some reluctance. He kissed her on the cheek and walked past her, into the apartment.

"Wait till you see what I have brought for you—" he crossed to the table and started pulling cartons out of a grease-stained paper bag—"tender duckling, steamed with delicate spices, pressed into dainty cakes and served with a spicy plum sauce." He indicated a small covered cup. "Spicy plum sauce."

"Steve, I'm going *out* to dinner."

Steve looked at her, surprised, but recovered immediately. "You'll change your mind," he promised, "when you taste Chung How Ku's Singapore Noodles."

"I've got a job."

"Hey, terrific. We'll celebrate." He opened a second, smaller bag. "A wine of recent vintage." He checked the label in mock appraisal. "*Very* recent."

"I'm meeting some agency people."

"Fortune cookies so wise you will gasp to read them." He took out a fortune cookie and snapped it in two.

"Steve, I can't have dinner with you." She said it firmly, to make him listen.

He would not permit his spirits to sag. "Okay, wonton for one." He sat in the nearest chair. "I'll watch TV till you get home."

Jolene looked at him for a long moment. It wasn't easy to do what she had to do. She gestured in the direction of his apartment. "Home is over *there*. The rent was paid, the lock is off the door."

Steve looked at her unhappily. "But I thought—"

"I thought that's what you thought." She hesitated. But she couldn't let herself weaken. It was better, for both of them, to deal with the situation *now*. "Look, Steve, you're a terrific guy, and I like you. I like you a lot. But right now, I want some time with just me, for me. Do you understand?"

Steve shook his head numbly.

"There's things I want to do."

"I wouldn't stop you."

"Yes, you would. You're not just another guy. When I look at you, I see Christmas cards with kids' pictures on the front."

Steve just stared at her, confused and vulnerable. She looked away, crossed to the table and started putting things back in the paper bag. "You're someone to stay home with, to take care of—and I don't want to stay home right now. I've got some dreams of my own. I haven't given them a real chance."

"I could help you. We could help each other." There was desperation in his eyes and his voice.

"It wouldn't work that way." She handed him the filled bag.

"Look, I promise—"

"I don't want promises." She was firm. When he started to say something more, she cut him off. "There is no place for you in my life. Please, go back to your apartment."

There was a terrible silence. Jolene looked at the floor. Finally, Steve got to his feet and walked slowly to the door. He stopped there and turned back. "Could you open the door?" He indicated the stained bag. "My hand's a little greasy."

Jolene went to open the door, still avoiding eye contact.

"Thanks. Not just for that—"

"I know."

After he went out, Jolene leaned back against her door, miserable.

Steve walked past his apartment. He didn't want to be closed up, to sit in a chair and look at walls. He wanted some air, some space. He needed to keep moving.

At the corner of Grove and Bleecker, he dropped the bag of Chinese food into a trash can, then turned toward Broadway.

He didn't keep track of time or distance. He just kept walking and thinking. He thought about Jolene, and more. His whole life passed before him, the way it's supposed to happen to a drowning man. Was he drowning? He did feel like he was going under for the third time. His career wasn't working. His personal life wasn't working. His only success had been as someone else, a comic-book hero, and now that was over. Maybe he should try to get something out of it. Maybe he should make an announcement. "I'm your hero—me, Steve Nichols, unemployed actor." Would they believe him? Would they care? He'd be a talk-show freak for a while and then—

It was starting to get dark. He was tired. He walked into an empty schoolyard, climbed up into a jungle gym and just perched there. He wasn't feeling sorry for himself so much as he was trying to think what to do next. What could he do about

Steve Nichols? He was worn out with being a flop.

A couple of kids ran into the yard. They didn't see Steve, too busy with their own fantasy.

"I got you," one boy shouted. "You're dead."

"You can't kill me. I'm Captain Avenger." The second boy faced his enemy with cocky defiance.

"Captain Avenger can get killed."

"No, he can't."

"Then I don't have a chance. It's not fair."

The second boy considered that reasoning. "Okay, he can get killed." Then he added very quickly, "But he won't."

Steve, listening to their discussion, smiled to himself.

"I might be Captain Avenger when I grow up," the second boy declared thoughtfully, "*really* be him."

"You can't. There already is one."

"Yeah, but he'll get old. He'll have to retire. Then somebody else will have to be him."

Steve was reflective as he watched them walk away. "Give them what they want," he heard Walter say. "Give them the legend."

Chapter
Twelve

AN elevated train ground to a stop at a station in the Bronx, to discharge and take on passengers. It was midafternoon. Most of the people on the platform were housewives and elderly shoppers. Steve was among them, wearing coveralls. He stepped onto the last car and walked to the rear, where he sat across the aisle from Eddie. There was no sign of recognition.

The train started to move again, quickly picking up speed, roaring past buildings at a third-floor level.

A man at the front of the car stood and faced the passengers. A black kerchief was tied over the lower half of his face, like a Western outlaw. His dark eyes had a desperate, crazed look. A snub-nosed revolver was in his nervous hand. "Everybody up!" he shouted.

People looked at him with gasps of surprise and fear.

"Come on, *move.*"

They got out of their seats, clumsy with sudden panic. Steve moved back against the rear door and Eddie stood squarely in front of him.

"Get to the back." The holdup man waved his revolver wildly.

The passengers obeyed, happy enough to put distance between themselves and the gunman.

They pressed together as close to the rear of the car as possible.

The gunman pulled a fabric sack from inside his jacket and threw it on the floor. "Wallets, purses —in the bag."

A frightened woman at the front of the group picked up the sack, dropped in her worn leather handbag, then passed it to the person behind her.

"Come on," the gunman snarled. "I haven't got all day."

The sack reached Eddie, who dropped in a wallet.

"Okay, the last man bring it up here."

There was a moment's pause, then a sudden rush of air. The holdup man and the passengers all turned, startled.

Captain Avenger stood in the open doorway, as if he had just stepped in from the narrow platform on the rear of the car. With his hands on his hips and his hair blowing across his forehead, he looked damned impressive. "Whatever you say, tough guy." Steve took the sack from Eddie and started to move forward.

The gunman stepped back, stunned by this "unexpected" turn of events. "Captain Avenger!" he exclaimed.

The passengers moved into the spaces between the seats to let Captain Avenger pass. As he walked, he tied a knot in the top of the sack. The people were silent, but their eyes were filled with relief and gratitude.

"Stay where you are!" The gunman aimed the revolver.

"Don't you want your loot?" With a quick swing of his arm, Steve threw the sack. It hit the bandit below the knees and knocked him over. In a flash, Steve was on top of him. The two men rolled down the center of the car in a desperate wrestling match.

The gunman broke free but in doing so, the revolver slipped out of his hand. He ran to the rear of the car. Passengers scrambled out of his way.

Steve was close behind him. The two men picked up their flight by the open rear door, the sounds of their struggle lost in the roar of the rushing train. At a point, Steve fell. The upper part of his body was outside the car, his head over the tracks. The gunman lunged. Steve caught him in the midsection with both feet and threw him backwards. The man fell but recovered quickly. He ran back to the front of the car and grabbed up the sack of loot.

The train was coming into the next station, stopping. The man was at the door, ready to jump off. Steve got to him just as the doors opened, pulled him around and threw a fist at his jaw. The bandit fell back over the nearest seat.

A handful of people waiting to board the train stared in amazement at what they saw. A policeman came through the crowd. But it was not a real policeman. It was Anthony, in a police uniform.

"Stand back. Let me in here." He walked up to Steve. "All right, Captain Avenger, I'll take over."

"Thanks, officer. Lucky you were here."

Anthony snapped handcuffs on the holdup man and led him away. Steve held out the sack of loot to the grateful passengers. Impulsively, a woman kissed him on the cheek. He smiled and turned away.

As Steve stepped off the train, there were expressions of admiration from the crowd. "Keep it up!" someone shouted. "You're our man."

"Who *are* you?" a woman asked.

Steve looked at her, very serious. "It doesn't matter." He raised his voice to the crowd at large. "It doesn't matter who I am. It's the idea that's important. Believe that." He looked around at the people, eager that they get the message. Then, suddenly, he turned and hurried to the stairs that led from the platform to the street below.

A car was waiting that whisked him away from the scene.

At WNAT, a young newswriter was typing up a story for broadcast. Gloria Preston came in and read over his shoulder. He looked back at her.

"Big C. A. has really done it this time," he grinned.

"So I heard." As she read the copy, Gloria shook her head wonderingly. "How the hell is somebody 'suddenly there' on a moving train?"

"Twenty witnesses say so, that's how."

Gloria read on. " 'It's the idea that's important.' "

"He stopped to make a speech, after it was all over."

"Hmm." Her eyes narrowed. "Seems like I've heard that speech before." She started to smile. Yes, she had heard it before, and she remembered where. She turned suddenly and started out of the room.

The young writer watched her go, shrugged and went back to his work.

Walter Reeves looked up, surprised, when Steve walked in unannounced. Walter's secretary, agitated, was half a dozen steps behind. "Mr. Reeves, I told him I'd have to check with you—"

Walter waved her away. "Don't worry about it." After the secretary was gone, he smiled at his unexpected visitor. "Sit down."

"No, thanks. I won't be here long."

A flicker of concern crossed Walter's face, but he kept smiling. "I hear we were a hit."

"Yeah. A smash. I'm not doing it anymore."

Walter frowned. What the hell did it mean, and how was he going to handle it?

Steve continued. "I told myself all those things were true, about the people needing Captain Avenger, about going out a legend—"

"And?" Walter fixed Steve with a firm, demanding gaze. "What else?"

"And I wanted a part in a play," Steve admitted. "I wanted to be somebody." He breathed a sigh and looked away for a moment, embarrassed by that truth.

"And what's the harm in doing something good for yourself?" Walter asked evenly. The first thing he had to do was get Steve to calm down.

"The harm is, I feel crappy. When I did it before, I felt good. Not this time."

Walter kept his voice and manner quiet, considerate. "Look, Steve, you've had a big day. Think this over and we'll talk again."

Steve shook his head.

"We've got an agreement. Remember?"

"I haven't collected my part," Steve answered and turned to go.

"Wait." Walter got up and walked around his desk. He couldn't let Steve go out that door. "The mayor's office has been in touch with me. About a ceremony at City Hall. Captain Avenger Day."

Steve was wary.

"There'll be television coverage, so everyone gets to see you. A nice way to end it, if you have to end it."

Steve thought about it. He didn't want to be part of any more hoaxes. But this wouldn't be a hoax. He was *the* Captain Avenger after all. Why not make one last appearance and do something worthwhile with it? "Give them the legend"— that was still a legitimate idea, no matter what kind of self-interest prompted it.

"All right," he submitted. "I'll do it."

Walter smiled.

"But that'll be it—the last time I put on that suit." He reached for the door.

"I'll let you know the details. And I'll send a car."

"I'll get there on my own."

"I'd rather send a car."

"Just let me know when and I promise you I'll be there." Steve walked out.

Walter walked back to his desk and called Calvin Donnelly. They congratulated each other on the elevated-train caper. Then Walter smoothly suggested that no further setups would be necessary. He'd like to go forward with plans for a Captain Avenger Day, built around a ceremony at City Hall.

Donnelly wasn't sure. It seemed premature.

"Trust me," said Walter.

Steve unlocked the door to his apartment and started to go in.

"You're crazy. Do you know that?"

He looked around as Jolene came toward him from her apartment. "I've heard it a couple of times."

"Armed robbers on elevated trains." She was angry. "Have you decided you really are Captain Avenger?"

"I won't be doing it again."

"That's what you said last time. Maybe you can't help yourself. Maybe it's some kind of addiction."

"Come on—"

"I ought to turn you in, for your own good."

"You don't want to deal with me. You've got other things to do."

Jolene breathed a sigh. Her voice softened. "I should have expected that."

Steve shrugged.

"I haven't even seen you in the last week."

"I've been busy."

"Riding around on elevated trains."

"Tomorrow I'm leaping a tall building in a single bound."

"Wrong guy."

"I'm expanding."

They looked helplessly at each other. There was no in-between for them, no "just friends." That was clear, and they both regretted it.

"Okay." Jolene became very cool. "Go ahead and get yourself killed, if that's what you want. Just don't tell me about it." She marched off.

Steve stared after her. "Damn!" He went into his apartment and slammed the door.

Chapter
Thirteen

A huge crowd was gathered on the wide walk that led from City Hall to the street, spilling over into the park on either side. The media was out in force. There were mobile TV units in the street and cameras were here and there in the crowd. A platform had been cantilevered on the front steps of the building, behind which hung a banner proclaiming "Captain Avenger Day." The columned portico was draped in bunting. A band was playing. The atmosphere was festive.

On the platform, the mayor was standing with a number of officials, including Calvin Donnelly.

"We're running late," the mayor said edgily. "Where is he?"

"I'll check on it."

Donnelly moved over to Walter, who was standing in a less prominent position. "Well?"

Walter shrugged helplessly. "He said he'd be here."

Donnelly gave Walter a cold look, then went back to the mayor. "Maybe we'd better go ahead," he advised.

"Without him?"

"Wo don't know what's happened."

"You got me into this, Calvin."

"I'm sorry, Your Honor."

131

"I don't like it." The mayor shook his head unhappily and moved off.

"Ladies and gentlemen," a dignitary announced from the rostrum, "the mayor of New York City."

The crowd applauded noisily, anxious for the ceremony to start.

Jolene watched the television coverage from her apartment. When cameras panned the enormous crowd, she felt uneasy, an undefined sense of dread. It was too much, this whole Captain Avenger thing, out of hand. She was anxious for Steve.

"Through the years," the mayor began, "many heroes have been honored on these steps, none of them more extraordinary than the one we honor today. Truly a man of the people." He hesitated. "I wish he had seen fit to accept our tribute in person."

There was a general groan of disappointment.

"I can only hope that, wherever he is, he can hear our heartfelt expression of gratitude."

A great gasp rose from the crowd. The mayor frowned wonderingly. People were looking up, pointing, smiling.

Captain Avenger stood on the portico above the platform. He put up his arms in salute and a tremendous cheer went up in response.

On the platform, the mayor and the others craned their necks to see. Walter started to smile.

Steve climbed over the portico railing, to the tops of twin Doric columns and caught hold of some bunting. It tore under his weight and lowered him to the platform below. The crowd loved it.

As officials and policemen cleared a path, Steve walked up to the mayor and shook his hand.

"Thank you, Mr. Mayor," he said. Then, turning to the crowd, he spoke into a battery of microphones. "I hope you'll forgive me for dropping in like this."

There was laughter and applause.

"I don't want you to think I don't appreciate the honor you're paying me today, the mayor and all of you. But I didn't come here for that."

Walter and Donnelly exchanged a look. Donnelly was openly anxious. Walter affected complete confidence.

"I came because I have something to say, and this is a chance to say it to a lot of people all at once. I guess it sounds sort of funny, under the circumstances, but what I want to say is—well, that I don't really matter very much, who I am or where I came from."

The crowd had become respectfully quiet. Loud speakers Ping-Ponged Steve's voice all over the park and out to the street, where vendors stopped hawking ice cream and cold drinks to listen.

"It doesn't matter if I ever show up again. It's what Captain Avenger stands for that's important. Justice and loyalty and courage—those things still exist. And there are heroes everywhere, if you look for them. Not guys with flashy suits and comic-book names. Just people, next door and down the block. People putting themselves on the line for other people. That's what being a hero is."

Jolene leaned toward her television set, her eyes shining. He was wonderful, this nut from Cawker City, wonderfully brave and unselfish and good. She was deeply proud of him.

"It's a kid risking his life to keep his little sister from getting hit by a truck. It's a guy that coaches Little League and hangs in there when he's tired and his head aches and he's worried about losing his job. It's being more than you have to be, taking a risk, getting involved."

He stopped to take a breath and wiped his face on his sleeve. He was starting to show the strain he was under, the pressure of the occasion. "Pay attention to heroes," he urged. "To everyday, next-door heroes. Believe in them. Be one yourself. Take a chance. What if we all did? What a world!" He took a moment to look out at the silent crowd, at the upturned faces. He smiled shyly. "That's all I have to say. But—well, I think it's a lot. Anyway, thanks for listening."

Steve turned from the rostrum. The crowd was suddenly alive with cheers and applause. The band started to play "The Sidewalks Of New York." The mayor, smiling broadly, pressed close to shake Steve's hand and give him an engraved plaque. Photographers moved in, their strobes flashing. Near the platform, where they would be caught by television cameras, a number of signs popped up: "New York loves Mayor Woodson and Captain Avenger. What a team!" Some of the signs carried pictures of both the mayor and the superhero. Steve frowned at the blatant use of the Captain Avenger image and name. The mayor raised his free hand, accepting the cheers of the crowd for himself.

Steve looked around unhappily, anxious to get away from what had become a political rally. Behind him, other officials were lining up, eager to shake his hand and get in on the act. Suddenly, he pulled away from the mayor, went to the edge of the platform and jumped off.

There was a gasp of surprise from the crowd and then a surge forward.

The mayor, Donnelly and Walter were astonished and angry. "What the hell is he doing?" Donnelly wondered aloud.

Steve faced the crowd. "Will you let me through?" he asked softly.

The closest people started to step aside, making way for him. As he moved into the crowd, it parted like the Red Sea. Some people reached out to take his hand for a moment, or just to touch him. A few women kissed him. But no one tried to stop him or hassle him in any way.

A car pulled up to the WNAT mobile unit and Gloria Preston got out. Two men stayed in the car. One was short and swarthy, the elevated train bandit. Gloria hurried up to the WNAT reporter who was covering Captain Avenger Day. He was on camera, talking into a hand mike: "It's difficult to see from here, but apparently Captain Avenger is walking through the center of this large crowd."

"Give me the mike," Gloria ordered.

The reporter turned away from camera. "Like hell."

She nodded toward the car. "Check with the station manager." She took the microphone and pushed her way into the crowd, trying to get to the walk that came down from City Hall. The cameraman followed.

"Captain Avenger, over *here!*"

Steve came closer, nodding to people, smiling.

"Gloria Preston, from WNAT."

Steve glanced at the reporter, who was now

only a few feet away. There was a moment of doubt, then recognition.

"How about a few words, Captain Avenger, for our viewers at home?"

He started to go off at another angle, away from her.

Gloria's expression hardened. "Over here, Steve."

He stopped to look back. Behind his mask, his eyes reflected a feeling not of fear but of sorrow, of deep regret. This reporter was going to ruin it and there was nothing he could do. He shook his head and started walked again.

Gloria began talking into the mike. "Ladies and gentlemen, there's a special reason I want to speak with Captain Avenger. I have learned his identity."

People nearby turned to look at her. She was addressing herself to the TV audience, but the close crowd could hear. "That's right, I know who New York's superhero really is. A small-time, unsuccessful actor named Steve Nichols, performing rehearsed heroics to sell a movie—and maybe a politician."

Word spread like wildfire. Captain Avenger was a fake! Other reporters picked it up and told their own audiences of Gloria's charges.

On the platform there was bewilderment and concern. Something was going on in the crowd, but they didn't know what. Then the mayor's press secretary, his face drained of color, brought a transistor TV that carried a picture of Gloria Preston somewhere out in that mass of people.

"The elevated-train robbery was staged," she reported. "The holdup man was as phony as Captain Avenger himself."

"Jesus Christ on a stick!" moaned Walter. He and Calvin Donnelly looked tensely at each other.

The crowd surged toward Steve. He looked back at Gloria in a baffled, heartsick way. Didn't she realize what she was doing, what she was taking away?

"Is it true?" a man called to him.

"Was it a fake?" someone else demanded.

Some of the people were just confused. Others were openly hostile.

"Not in the beginning," Steve tried to explain. "But later—"

"It's true," a woman said sadly. "He admits it."

"I let them use me, because I wanted something so much."

"It was all a con!" a man declared angrily.

"No. Listen. What it stood for—I believed in that, from the first. I still do. Please listen to me."

"Let him talk," someone pleaded.

"We've heard enough!"

Arguments began to break out in the crowd. Some pushing started.

Steve tried to shout above the general confusion. "It doesn't matter what you think of me. But don't forget the idea."

An ice-cream bar hit the side of his face and ran down onto his costume. There was more pushing. He fell back. Someone grabbed at his cape. It tore. Police broke through and shoved people away from him. A fight started. Confusion threatened to become chaos. Steve broke loose and ran. There was nothing else he could do.

On the platform, the mayor, shaken, went back to the microphones. "My fellow New Yorkers, if what I have just heard is true, I am as appalled and disappointed as any of you—"

Donnelly came up to him. "The mikes are off. We'd better go inside."

"Where's the car?" Walter asked Eddie.

"Follow me."

As Gloria Preston tried to get back to the mobile unit, she was bumped and pushed, caught in the turmoil she had created. She passed an old man seemingly oblivious to what was happening around him, tears running down his cheeks. It was the bum Steve had talked to outside Sardi's, the first person told about Captain Avenger.

Jolene turned off her television set. Tears were on her cheeks too.

Chapter
Fourteen

THAT night, a small crowd of people, curiosity seekers, hung around Twenty-six Grove Street. On the front steps, a knot of newsmen and photographers waited for some new development, a new piece of information, anything at all that could be built into a story.

Jolene, who had been hounded by reporters, at her door and on the telephone, tried to leave the building and was surrounded. Cameras flashed in her face. Microphones were thrust at her.

"When did you first meet him?"

"Do you expect him to contact you?"

"I don't know *what* to expect. I don't know anything." Jolene put her hand in front of her face.

"What do you think about him being a fraud, or did you know that before today?"

"Some people think he should be arrested. Do you agree with that?"

"Arrested?" She couldn't believe what she was hearing.

"Did you know a PR firm was telling him what to do?"

"No."

"Just how close were you?"

She pulled back, shaking her head, overwhelmed by the crush of people, the barrage of questions.

"Did you ever suspect him of being a phony? A con artist?"

"He wasn't," she said quietly.

"What did she say?"

"Speak up!"

Suddenly Jolene straightened. Her voice became firm and clear. "He wasn't a phony."

"Huh? Is she kidding?"

"The person I knew was real. The bullet wound in his arm was real. I know, I bandaged it. And what he believed in, that was real too."

"Are you going to defend what he did?"

"That's all I have to say." She turned to go back in the front door. When a reporter blocked her, she looked him straight in the eye. "Mister," she warned, "I've got a mean knee. If you don't want to sing soprano—"

Getting the message, the man stepped aside. Jolene went back to her apartment, slammed the door and took the phone off the hook.

It was hours later when the last newsman left and the street was quiet. A lone figure, dressed in a shabby hat and overcoat, approached and entered the building. Not far away, a siren screamed through the night.

Steve moved quietly to his apartment, unlocked his door and stepped in. He turned on a light, went straight to the closet, pulled out a suitcase and opened it on the bed. He pulled off the tattered coat he had taken from a rubbish bin and dropped it on the floor. When there was a knock on the door, he stiffened apprehensively.

"Steve?" It was Jolene's voice.

He hesitated a moment, then went to open the door.

"I was watching for you." She looked in his eyes and saw something she had never seen there before: defeat. It broke her heart. "I'm sorry," she said softly.

"I got what I deserve." He turned from the door. "I gave them something, and then I took it away."

Jolene followed him into the apartment. "You're being pretty tough on yourself."

"Just trying to be honest."

Steve opened drawers and started throwing things in the suitcase.

"If you run away, the bad guys win."

"They will anyway. They've got the numbers."

"I don't know. Maybe there's more of you than you think. Fight back. Keep talking."

"Nobody listens."

"I did."

He looked at her.

"If we don't get something sooner, try us later."

Steve considered that for a moment, then shook his head and went back to his packing.

Jolene sighed unhappily. "What about your career?"

"Some career."

"You're going to give up acting? You're going to let them take that away from you too?"

"Maybe they're doing me a favor. Maybe I'm not any good."

He went to the closet again, pulled out a jacket, some slacks and his trench coat.

"You did a pretty good job as Captain Avenger," Jolene pointed out.

"I couldn't sustain the character," he answered with a wry smile.

"How often do you get your costume pulled off in the middle of a performance? It's not fair."

Suddenly there was a crash, a shattering of glass, a tearing of window shade. A brick hit the floor. Steve moved quickly to turn off the light. Outside, there was the sound of running.

"My God!" Jolene's voice was trembling.

"When they start throwing things, it's time to get off," Steve said bitterly. "Any actor knows that." He shut the suitcase, pulled on his trench coat and went to the door. "You'd better get out of here," he said over his shoulder. "You could get hurt."

Tears glistened in Jolene's eyes. There was more than one way to get hurt.

Steve looked back at her. "Good luck with—well, with all the things you want." He went out into the hall and started walking toward the front door.

Jolene followed him. "What about the things *you* want?"

"I'm not sure what they are anymore."

"I don't believe that."

Steve walked out of the apartment building and looked in both directions. No one was near. In the distance, there was a chorus of sirens. He went down the steps to the sidewalk.

Jolene came to the door. "All right, give up. Go back to Cawker City and lick your wounds!" She was sad and angry, and desperate. "Forget your career. Forget Captain Avenger. And forget *me*. Let the whole world go to hell!"

Steve looked back at her.

A window opened. "What's all the noise out here?"

"Oh, shut up!" Jolene yelled.

Mrs. Havachek pulled back, astonished. Steve started to walk on.

"I'll forget too," Jolene called after him. "I'll forget I ever met you. We'll *all* forget you. We can, you know. We can forget anything!"

She stood there for a moment, rigid, then turned and went back inside.

A fire truck went through the nearest intersection, its air horns blasting a warning.

Steve walked toward the corner, slowly at first, then faster. He looked up the cross street, as police cars whizzed past. An area two blocks away was crowded with police vehicles, ambulances and fire engines. There was a great rumbling, like thunder, but more ominous.

Jolene stood by the mailboxes, just inside the front door, letting tears run freely down her face. She looked up, reacting to the strange rumble, as it culminated in a kind of roar. Looking through the glass of the door, she saw people in the street, hurrying toward the corner. Lights came on in other buildings, as people were roused from their sleep. Curious, she went back outside.

Steve saw flames leap and heard orders shouted on a bullhorn. He moved toward the confusion. People around him, their attention similarly focused, paid no attention to him.

Searchlights played on an old brick building. One side had collapsed into a heap of brick and wood and broken furniture. Rooms were exposed on every floor. Firemen were in an area where a line had burst and escaping gas had ignited.

Television reporters and cameramen moved as close to the building as permitted. They wandered among dazed tenants who had fled or been rescued. Some were being treated on the spot for injuries.

A TV newsman was filming a report, his commentary fast-paced and dramatic: "Police and fire department spokesmen have made an announcement that all occupants were removed from the building in fast action by both departments. Some forty persons have been taken to nearby hospitals. It is estimated that another thirty or forty have received medical treatment on the scene."

There was a groaning noise in the building, then the breaking of strained timbers. A rescue squad hurried out the front entrance, as some inner walls collapsed with a thunderous crash. The entire structure shuddered.

"There goes still another section of the building. Rescuers making a final check after that *last* collapse got out just in time."

Steve was among onlookers being held back by police, awed by what he was watching.

Gloria Preston faced a camera: "An investigation will start immediately to determine the cause of the cave-in. It has been suggested that demolition activity less than a block away put new stress on a structure already weakened by age and neglect, triggering this disaster."

Among the last out of the building were two

firemen with a woman on a stretcher. Dazed and disoriented, she raised herself up and twisted around to take another look. "Johnny?" Suddenly, the name became a scream. "Johnny!"

The firemen tried to calm her, but she wouldn't be calmed. Her eyes darted here and there, desperately searching. "I don't see him! Oh, my God!"

The Fire Chief walked over to her. "What is it?"

"My baby! He's still in there!"

The chief turned to the rescue team. "You just brought her out?"

They nodded. From the third floor. But they didn't see a child.

Just then, the building was rocked by an explosion. Flames shot high in the air. The woman, horrified, tried to get off the stretcher, to go back to the building. The firemen restrained her.

"No one can go in there now," the Fire Chief told her. "It's too dangerous."

"Maybe somebody else got your boy," one of the firemen offered.

The woman put her face in her hands, moaning.

Jolene stood at the back of the crowd of onlookers, trying to see through.

Gloria Preston continued her report: "There is now some doubt that everyone has been removed from the building. But all rescue efforts have been stopped because of the imminent danger of further explosions and collapse. Fire and rescue crews have been ordered to stay out."

Someone in the crowd shouted and pointed up. "What's that?"

A searchlight found a figure poised on the roof of the building next door. He wore no mask or cape, but the red, blue and gold costume was unmistakable.

"It's Captain Avenger!"

He backed up, then ran forward and leaped from roof to roof.

Jolene pressed anxiously forward.

"Judas H. Priest!" exclaimed Gloria, prompting the cameraman to remind her she was on the air.

A hush fell over the crowd, as they continued to watch the building.

Steve moved through that part of the building that was not in flames. Walls were sagging, ceilings broken. Plaster dust was falling all around him. He climbed over rubble, looking and listening. There was an ominous creaking sound. The building seemed to sway slightly, then was still again. A cry came from somewhere. Steve turned in its direction.

The crowd kept watching, tense and quiet. Even the newsmen had fallen silent, letting their cameras tell the story of what was happening.

Jolene had worked her way to the front of the crowd, where a policeman stopped her.

Inside the building, Steve hurried down a broken stairway, from the fourth floor to the third. There was more creaking. An exposed pipe broke and there was a brief hiss of gas escaping. And again, the cry came, weak and frightened.

Following the sound, Steve pushed over a door and entered a kitchen filled with debris. There was movement in the corner. Steve pulled away some broken timbers. He looked up anxiously when the building groaned like some huge animal in pain, then went back to his work and suddenly looked into the dirty, tear-stained face of a boy. The child, who had taken refuge under the kitchen sink, looked at his rescuer in wonder. "Captain Avenger!"

Steve smiled and picked him up. He carried him into a room that was on the front of the building.

"He's got the kid!" All eyes in the crowd went to a third-floor window.

The child's mother raised her arms, crying and laughing at the same time. "Johnny! Johnny!"

Firemen rushed a net to just under the window. The Chief used a bullhorn to call directions. "Drop the child first, then jump yourself."

The boy clutched at Steve, frightened.

"It's okay, you'll be fine." Steve smiled reassuringly.

Still, the child clung.

"Do you trust me?"

The boy nodded.

"Then let go."

The boy released his hold and Steve dropped him. He landed safely in the net and was quickly lifted out. There were cheers from the crowd.

Steve sighed his relief and got ready to jump himself. But then, a great trembling began, as if the building had been caught in an earthquake. Steve was thrown down. A section of floor above gave way. He disappeared in smoke and debris.

The crowd was stunned into silence. Jolene pressed forward, anxiously calling his name. When the policeman restraining her looked toward the collapse, she broke past him. He went after her, caught her and pulled her back. "He's still alive in there!" she cried. "I know he is."

The policeman held stubbornly onto her. The crowd around them was quiet, looking up at the doomed building with their hero caught inside. Then, a tenant who escaped the cave-in unharmed, a burly middle-aged man, stepped forward. "I'm goin' in there," he declared.

A second policeman tried to stop him. "You can't."

"I'm goin' in," he repeated firmly.

Another man came out of the crowd. "Me, too."

"An amazing thing is happening," a newsman reported, "people are going into that building, risking their lives."

Gloria watched wonderingly, incredulous. "I'll be damned."

A couple of firemen, acting on their own, against orders, started into the building. The Chief stood at the entrance, after the first several people had entered, and pleaded with others to stay back. "Please. You might cause it to go."

The forward movement stopped, as people considered his warning. They waited and watched, quiet and solemn.

The rescuers moved into the area where Steve was caught by the collapse. They started to dig into the debris, pulling away timbers and hunks of plaster. They worked quickly and quietly. A fireman came on a flash of red. "Here!" he called excitedly.

They all turned to that place and began to dig. Steve, uncovered, groaned and opened his eyes.

"Are you all right?" one of his rescuers asked.

Steve looked around at these people who had come in to save him, who had risked their lives, and he started to smile.

The crowd continued to wait, hushed. The building was creaking like a ship in a heavy sea.

Jolene stood at the front of the crowd, hardly breathing.

The rescuers came out, with Steve at the center of the group. His head was cut and he was limping slightly, but he was all right. Jolene ran to him. He held her close.

The crowd was quiet. People didn't cheer or applaud. They smiled, and in their shining smiles there was more happiness than cheers could express.

As Steve and the others came away from the building, there was another terrible roar and a great crash, as the rest of the structure collapsed. The crowd stared in awe. For a long moment, there wasn't a sound. Then TV and newspaper reporters, regaining their customary aplomb, closed in on Steve with cameras and microphones. He stepped back from them, putting up his hands. Shaking his head, not responding to their questions, he looked around for a way out.

"Please," Jolene implored, "he's had enough."

Then something happened in the crowd. Without a word to each other, acting on a common impulse, people started to move. They got between Captain Avenger and the reporters, shielding him. They cordoned off a way for him to walk, unmolested, out of the area.

He looked at Jolene. "Let's go home, J."

"Cawker City?"

"No, home."

They started to walk the path cleared for them. As he went, Steve smiled and received smiles in return. The mother, her child in her arms, called after him, for everyone—"God bless you!"

Gloria Preston's cameraman turned to her. "It's him, isn't it? The same guy."

She stared after the departing hero. "I guess it doesn't make much difference. I guess it's the idea that's important."

Beyond the crowd, Steve and J walked off holding hands.

Bestsellers from BALLANTINE